"Are you saying I shouldn't try to find Emma?"

"I'm saying be careful."

A shot fired, the glass window shattered, and the reporter gasped. Blood oozed from his arm.

Lizzie screamed.

"Run." He pointed them toward the back door. "Through the kitchen. There's a rear exit. Go now so you can get a head start. Hurry."

Caleb grabbed Lizzie. They raced through the kitchen to the car and exited the parking area by way of the alley.

She glanced back. Another round of gunfire erupted.

Her heart pounded. "Are they following us?"

"I don't see anyone."

Caleb accelerated and turned north at the intersection. "We'll take the long route back to Pinecraft."

"Will we be safe there?"

"I'm not sure you'll be safe anywhere in the city. Like Jeb said, you need to get away before they catch you."

And if they caught her...what would happen then?

Debby Giusti is an award-winning Christian author who met and married her military husband at Fort Knox, Kentucky. Together they traveled the world, raised three wonderful children and have now settled in Atlanta, Georgia, where Debby spins tales of mystery and suspense that touch the heart and soul. Visit Debby online at debbygiusti.com, blog with her at seekerville.blogspot.com and craftieladiesofromance.blogspot.com, and email her at Debby@DebbyGiusti.com.

Books by Debby Giusti

Love Inspired Suspense

Her Forgotten Amish Past
Dangerous Amish Inheritance
Amish Christmas Search

Amish Witness Protection

Amish Safe House

Amish Protectors

Amish Refuge
Undercover Amish
Amish Rescue
Amish Christmas Secrets

Visit the Author Profile page at Harlequin.com for more titles.

AMISH CHRISTMAS SEARCH

DEBBY GIUSTI

LOVE INSPIRED SUSPENSE
INSPIRATIONAL ROMANCE

LOVE INSPIRED® SUSPENSE
INSPIRATIONAL ROMANCE

ISBN-13: 978-1-335-72198-3

Recycling programs
for this product may
not exist in your area.

Amish Christmas Search

Copyright © 2020 by Deborah W. Giusti

This edition published by arrangement with Harlequin Books S.A.

For questions and comments about the quality of this book, please contact us
at CustomerService@Harlequin.com.

Love Inspired
22 Adelaide St. West, 40th Floor
Toronto, Ontario M5H 4E3, Canada
www.Harlequin.com

Printed in U.S.A.

I will sing of the mercies of the Lord for ever:
with my mouth will I make known thy faithfulness
to all generations.
−Psalms 89:1

This story is dedicated to
doctors and medical professionals
who sacrifice their own well-being
to care for the sick and suffering,
especially those infected with
COVID-19.
May God bless them and keep them in His care.

ONE

"I'm running out of time," Lizzie Kauffman moaned as she reached for the polishing cloth and rubbed it over the silver teapot. Her housekeeping job at Thad Thompson's estate in Sarasota, Florida, would end Saturday, and she had yet to find information about Mr. Thompson's twenty-five-year-old adoptive son, Andrew.

The memory of what had happened three years ago continued to haunt her. The police had been convinced Andrew was out of the country the night her best friend, Emma Bontrager, had gone missing.

With a heavy heart, Lizzie regarded her own reflection staring back at her as the silver began to shine. She knew the truth about that night, but law enforcement had failed to listen when a young Amish girl on vacation with her family claimed the son of one of Sarasota's most prominent businessmen had kidnapped her friend.

Once the teapot gleamed, she returned it to the sideboard and swiped the cloth over the sugar bowl. If only the memory could be wiped away as easily as the tarnish.

What had happened troubled Lizzie, filling not only her dreams but also her waking hours with unanswered questions about Emma. Eventually, Lizzie had left her family and her Amish community in the North Georgia mountains and made her way back to Sarasota, spurred on by the need for closure. In spite of the odds and grateful that her name had never been released to the media, "Elizabeth" Kauffman had wrangled one housekeeping job after another until fate—or *Gott*—had seemingly led her to the housekeeping agency that eventually resulted in temporary employment at the Thompson residence. Exactly where she needed to be in case Andrew came home.

Lost in the painful memory, Lizzie startled as the door leading from the Thompson dining room swung open, pulling her back to the present as Nadine Cavanaugh stepped into the kitchen. Like Lizzie, the other housekeeper was dressed in a blue shirtwaist uniform and white apron.

"My feet are killing me," the older woman lamented. "But I finished ironing the damask cloth and placed it on the table for Saturday's announcement party."

Approaching the sideboard where Lizzie had arranged the pieces of silver she had already polished, Nadine nodded her head in approval. "You're doing a fine job. How long before you're finished?"

"The tray's my last piece. I just need to tidy Mr. Thompson's office before I call it a night."

"He should give you an early Christmas bonus,

hard as you've been working." Nadine tsked. "Course, I doubt that will happen."

The doorbell chimed.

Nadine wrinkled her brow. "Who would be stopping by this late at night?"

Lizzie dropped her polishing cloth. "Mr. Thompson's in the library. I'll get the—"

Nadine held up her hand. "Keep working. I'll answer the door before I leave. See you tomorrow."

Hearing Nadine open the front door, Lizzie reached for the silver tray and rubbed it with the polishing cloth.

Moments later, the door slammed shut with a *bang*. Heavy footsteps crossed the grand foyer and headed to the library in the south wing of the stately home.

Nadine scurried back to the kitchen, eyes wide and concern written over her weathered face. "Andrew's come home."

Lizzie's heart lurched. "Mr. Thompson's son?"

Nadine nodded. "The black sheep of the family, and I'm not spreading gossip. I'm telling the truth. Mr. Thompson adopted Andrew after he and Mrs. Thompson married, but that boy always gave him a hard time. After Mrs. Thompson passed, everything got worse."

The older housekeeper lowered her voice. "From the smell of him, Andrew's liquored up and ready to pick a fight with his dad. I don't like you staying behind when he's in the house. You want me to help you finish?"

"Go home to your family. I'm done polishing and will be right behind you."

"Bless you, child, but be careful. Don't rile Mr. Andrew when he's drinking." She shook her head. "He gets nasty mean when he's under the influence. You sure you're okay?"

"Go on, Nadine. I won't be long."

The woman waved a farewell and continued to mumble under her breath as she left the house through the back door.

Lizzie had to work quickly. Since her first day of employment at the Thompson estate, she had been watching and waiting, but Andrew had never shown up nor had his father mentioned his wayward son, as if Andrew had disappeared that night along with Emma. Over the last few weeks, Lizzie had come to the painful conclusion that her search might have been for naught.

Now that Andrew had returned home, she needed to learn as much as she could about where he had been and what he had been doing for the last three years. If only he would also provide a clue to Emma's disappearance.

After arranging the coffee-and-tea service on the silver tray, she carried it into the dining room and placed it on the buffet table decorated with red bulbs and Christmas greenery. The door to the library hung open.

Mr. Thompson's voice floated through the foyer to where Lizzie was standing. "I told you to stay on the island, Andrew."

Her pulse quickened. Getaway Island, located off the coast of Florida, was owned by Mr. Thompson. She had researched his holdings, including the lush tropical resort.

"It's been three years," Andrew shot back. "The police have other people to investigate. Besides, you can't run my life forever."

"As long as I'm paying your bills, you'll do what I say." Mr. Thompson raised his voice even more. "Is that understood?"

Lizzie imagined the younger man staring at his father with defiance.

"I'm announcing my candidacy for the senate at a small gathering of my most influential supporters here on Saturday night," Mr. Thompson continued. "I don't want anything to spoil the evening so keep a low profile, Andrew, and stay out of trouble. We've got a problem brewing with that woman, and I don't want anything you do now to cause the cops to review what happened three years ago."

Moaning inwardly, Lizzie raised her hand to her heart, knowing instinctively he was talking about Emma.

Andrew chuckled. "*Wish* woman?"

"You mean *which* one?" Mr. Thompson scoffed. "You're drunk, Andrew, and slurring your words. Your mother ensured the Amish girl was cared for, but she would come back and haunt us both if she knew about the others."

Had more women disappeared?

"The island security guards look the other way because of the monthly bonuses I provide." Mr. Thompson huffed. "But your first mishap here on the mainland has me worried. Your uncle's worried too."

Lizzie moved into the foyer and closer to the library.

"What's the problem?" For the first time, Andrew sounded concerned.

"She's starting to remember. As if that's not enough, the state inspectors are snooping around. They suspect Medicaid fraud after finding some discrepancies in the billing system. Warren wants to sell the nursing home."

Andrew laughed nervously. "Uncle Warren answers to you, Dad. Or did you forget who owns the facility?"

"If the woman talks—"

"She can't incriminate me." Bluster punctuated Andrew's less than emphatic response.

"Because you beat her to a pulp and almost killed her."

Lizzie let out an inaudible gasp and blinked back tears, determined not to cry.

Mr. Thompson's voice was ripe with accusation as he continued, "I've got this month's bill on my desk and have a mind to make you pay for her care."

"She teased me," Andrew whined. "And egged me on that night."

"She was seventeen, Andy, and Amish."

A lump filled Lizzie's throat.

"Your mother said her long-term care was our responsibility, but your mother's gone and I've had enough of your tomfoolery."

"Don't worry, Dad. I'll put an end to the problem."

Emma wasn't the problem Lizzie wanted to scream. Andrew was.

"Your uncle's going on vacation after a rehabilitation symposium we're both taking part in at the end of the week. I'll fly home Saturday afternoon for the party that evening. Wait until Warren has left the area and I'm back in Florida before you do anything. Don't mess this up, Andrew. If you make a mistake, I'll disavow knowledge of her, as well as you."

"You disowned me years ago."

"If not for your mother, I might have. Although she's gone, so nothing's holding me back now. Do this right, Andy, and we'll continue to keep in touch. Make a mistake and you're no longer my son."

"I don't know why mother married you?"

"Like you, she probably wanted my money. Now get out of here."

"Only after you open the safe."

"What?"

"I deserve a hefty bonus for my hard work on the island."

Mr. Thompson jeered. "The resort was better served before I gave you the assistant manager job."

Lizzie's chest tightened. If she had the nursing home's address, she could find Emma.

Pulse racing, she hurried into Mr. Thompson's office, eased the door closed behind her and shuffled through the papers on his desk. In her haste, she failed to see the brass letter opener that dropped to the floor. She stooped to retrieve the heavy object.

Her breath caught as she heard the office door open. Rising upright, she turned. Her heart nearly stopped. Andrew Thompson towered in the doorway. The hateful man Emma had gone off with that night stood six-two, with collar-length brown hair and piercing eyes that widened with surprise.

Mr. Thompson pushed past his son. "You're still here, Elizabeth?"

"The silver, sir. I was polishing—"

"She heard us." Andrew was beside her that fast. He grabbed her arm. His fingers dug into her flesh. His breath reeked of alcohol and his eyes flashed with anger.

"Where's Emma?" she demanded. "I thought

you killed her, but if she's alive, I'm going to find her."

He slapped her face. Lizzie reeled backward. Her hip crashed into the desk. Pain shot along her spine.

"Andrew, no!" Mr. Thompson stepped between them.

His son shoved him aside. The older man fell to the floor.

Andrew wrapped his hands around Lizzie's neck.

She gasped.

Mr. Thompson tried to stand. "Stop, Andrew."

"She was with Emma that night."

"What!" His father's eyes widened, his face reddened.

Andrew's grasp tightened. "I'll take care of both of them."

Struggling to pull free of his hold, Lizzie raised the letter opener and stabbed his neck.

"*Augh!*" He dropped his hands and fell back. Blood spewed from the puncture wound.

Fear clutched her heart. She moaned, frozen in time.

A warning sounded in her head. *Run!*

Without another moment's hesitation, she fled the office, crossed the foyer, dashed into the kitchen and out the back door. The cool night air greeted her.

Glancing down at her right hand, she saw blood

on her fingers. Andrew's blood. Her stomach roiled with revulsion. She wiped her hand over her apron and raced across the expansive porch. Her feet tripped down the steps. She caught herself and ran along the servants' drive.

"Alert security," Mr. Thompson's voice bellowed from inside the house.

Lizzie's heart pounded so hard she feared it would explode. She saw her bike, grabbed the handlebars and pushed off, her feet pumping as fast as they could go.

The rear gate hung open. A roar filled her ears as she zipped through the wrought iron opening, crossed the street and headed onto a back road. Less than a minute later, a security car pulled out of the property and onto the street almost directly behind her.

She peddled faster. Mr. Thompson would do anything to protect his reputation, especially when he was set to announce his candidacy. The only thing that would stop his rise to power was Andrew. His wild living and hunger for young women would wreck his father's political aspirations.

Emma was alive!

Tears of relief burned Lizzie's eyes along with concern for what her friend had endured. Andrew had beaten her? Lizzie's heart broke, thinking how Emma must have suffered.

She wiped her cheeks and swallowed hard.

Headlights crawled over her. She glanced back, seeing the security vehicle, its bright light on the roof flashing. She turned into a nearby driveway and peddled around the ranch-style A-frame house bedecked with Christmas lights, through the green space and the neighboring property on the next street.

At the corner, she turned east, cut behind a gas station and sped along an alleyway.

A dog barked. *Keep him at bay*, she silently prayed to *Gott*, whom she had ignored for too long.

A siren sounded. Its shrill scream in the dark night shoved her heartbeat up a notch. Bile rose in her throat. She pushed on until her hands ached from gripping the handlebars and the calves of her legs burned with fatigue.

Her apartment was nearby, but that was the first place Mr. Thompson's men would look.

What about law enforcement? Would security notify the police, and would they be waiting for her at home? Mouth dry, head pounding, she steered onto a narrow two-lane.

The nearby highway was awash with flashing lights as if every law-enforcement agency in the surrounding area had been called in. An accident or were they searching for her?

If so, she didn't have a chance.

Unless she laid low until the frenzy of their search died down. A hiding place came to mind.

Some distance away, but she was determined to find shelter and safety at least for tonight.

The ride took longer than she remembered from her youth. The sound of a car's engine caused her to turn. Headlights caught Lizzie in their glare. A siren screamed to life. She peddled into another alleyway, then along a dirt path and through a backyard, fearing what would happen if security found her.

Andrew's words played through her mind. "I'll take care of both of them."

Turning onto a narrow road, she crossed Phillippi Creek. Pinecraft Park was on her right. She hurried along Fry Street, passed Good Avenue and turned onto a side street. In her mind's eyes, she saw Emma flirting with a young Amish man at the park during one of the evening singings. Later that same night, she and Emma had giggled to themselves and dreamed of the future.

The future was now, with all its terrible reality.

Her shoulders and legs burned, but she needed to find her hiding place. She turned right, then left. Surely security wouldn't look for her holed up in one of the houses usually rented to Amish families who bused south for a winter vacation before spring planting. This close to Christmas, a number of the small cottages sat dark and unoccupied.

Gasping, she entered the backyard of the house her own family had often rented and latched the gate behind her. She shoved her bike behind a row of oleander shrubs, found the large garden stone exactly where it had been three years ago, lifted it off the ground and dug in the dirt. Her fingers found the key.

Working quickly, she brushed off the sandy soil and hurried to the back door. Sirens drew closer. Her gut tightened.

With trembling hands, Lizzie opened the screen door, stuck the key in the lock and turned the knob.

"Who's there?" A male voice, deep, demanding.

Her heart stopped.

She recognized the voice, but how—

He stepped to the doorway. Even in the darkness, she could see his bulk and the outline of his angled jaw.

The squeal of sirens neared. Lights flashed. A car turned at the corner and braked to a stop. Shouts sounded in the night.

Fear lodged in her throat. She stared at the man in the doorway, her voice little more than a whisper when she spoke.

"Help—help me, Caleb."

He hesitated for half a heartbeat, then grabbed her arm and yanked her inside. He closed the door, engaged the lock and pulled her tight against him, his lips to her ear.

"Be silent, Lizzie, so they do not hear you."

Growing up, she had always felt safe with Caleb Zook, but tonight, with the security guards shouting outside, she doubted anyone—even the man who had planned to marry Emma Bontrager—could save her.

Caleb never thought he would see Lizzie again after he left the North Georgia mountains and turned his back on the Amish community.

How had she found him? And why?

A knock sounded at the front door.

Knowing she was in danger, Caleb hurried her into a spare bedroom. "Do not make a sound."

He ruffled his hair, untucked his white shirt, lowered one suspender over his arm and kicked off his shoes.

The knock came again, followed by an insistent pounding that nearly shook the house.

"Patience," Caleb grumbled under his breath.

He inched the door open and feigned a yawn. "*Yah*?"

"We're looking for a woman on a bicycle who may have entered this area. Five-five, dark hair, brown eyes." The guy held up his cell.

Lizzie stared back at Caleb from the screen on the man's phone. She appeared to be running from a stately home and looked scared.

Caleb scrubbed his hand over his face and chuckled as he pointed to the picture. "The only place I would have seen this pretty woman is in my dreams."

"Look, buddy. Don't play games with me."

"I am not playing, but I *am* hoping to return to my bed as soon as possible."

"What about your neighbors? No one's answering their doors."

"It is December, *yah*? Pinecraft will draw more visitors after Christmas."

"Yet you're here," the guy sneered.

"I work in the area."

"If you see this woman—" the guy pointed again to Lizzie's picture, then jammed a business card into Caleb's hand "—call my number."

Estate Security.

"She has done something wrong?" Caleb asked.

"You got that right. Happened little over an hour ago. Stabbed a guy in the neck and forced him to open his safe."

"She does not sound like someone from Pinecraft. Most people in this neighborhood are peace-loving Amish."

"Amish or *Englisch*," the guy snarled. "We need to find her. Watch your back. She's dangerous."

The guard hurried on to the next house. Caleb eyed the four men, wearing khaki slacks and navy shirts, who continued to knock on doors. Eventually, they headed back to their car. As they drove away, Caleb stepped into the cottage and locked the door behind him.

Hearing footsteps, he turned to see Lizzie in the hallway, her face pale, her lips drawn.

"Why did you come here?" he demanded.

"I… I never thought the house would be rented this close to Christmas."

Caleb pulled in a deep breath, checked that the curtains were drawn and then flipped on a small light. He glanced at the uniform she wore. His chest tightened.

Stepping closer, he pointed to the streaks of blood that covered her apron. "Are you hurt?"

She glanced down and groaned. Her left hand reached for a nearby chair as if to steady herself. "Someone grabbed me. I had to protect myself."

Pulling in a deep breath, she untied her apron, dropped it into the trash can near the kitchen sink and washed her hands over and over again as if trying to cleanse herself from what had happened.

When she turned back to him, her eyes were wide, her mouth drawn. "I need to stay here tonight, Caleb. I'll leave in the morning."

Growing up in the North Georgia mountains, Lizzie had been energetic with an adventurous spirit. As the years passed, she had become more levelheaded and deliberate in her actions. Tonight was different. Without a shadow of a doubt, she was in danger and unable to think beyond the moment.

He lowered his voice. "Where will you go?"

She shook her head. "I'm not sure, Caleb, but I do not want to cause any more problems. I've already hurt you enough."

Hurt me? He wanted to ask what she meant, but he saw the raw emotion in her gaze and the way her shoulders slumped with fatigue. He would brew a pot of coffee and feed her, as well as provide lodging for the night. Or as long as she needed refuge.

As much as he did not want to get involved, he could not stand by and do nothing to help Lizzie. He owed her that much. The three of them—he and Lizzie and Emma Bontrager—had been close friends who explored the hillsides together, fished in the river and often speculated about the future. Emma had been the flirt who seemed confident of his attention, while Lizzie had grown reserved and careful not to show her feelings as they aged. Especially when Emma was in one of her moods. Caleb appreciated the thoughtful way Lizzie approached life, but their friendship had been torn apart the night Emma went missing.

For the last three years, Caleb had tried to forget his own role in Emma's disappearance. The day she had gone missing, she had asked when they would marry. Her brazenness had rocked him to the core, especially since he had done nothing to make her think he cared for her in a romantic way. Unsettled by her remark, he had explained that marriage wasn't in their future. Her shocked expression and the way she had turned away from him in a huff was proof enough that Emma had gone to the beach on the rebound, in hopes Caleb would reconsider his plans for the future. All this time, he had tried to bury his own guilt in throwing her off balance that day. How ironic that now, because of Lizzie, he was once again face-to-face with the past.

The *Englisch* said *Gott* had a sense of humor, but Caleb was not laughing.

TWO

The Pinecraft cottage brought back visions of Lizzie's family gathered around the kitchen table where she now sat. The memories cut into her heart and made what she had just endured seem even more surreal.

Caleb placed a mug of coffee on the table in front of her. Inhaling the aroma of the fresh ground beans, she wrapped her hand around the warm mug and took a sip of the rich brew.

"Good coffee." Her voice sounded drained of emotion even to her own ears, as if she had spent her last bit of energy and had nothing else to give.

Tall and muscular, Caleb stood with his back to the counter and watched her, his dark brown eyes filled with questions. He wanted answers that she would provide as soon as her trembling eased and she could think rationally again.

Hoping to bide her time, she glanced at the electric coffee maker and the overhead kitchen lighting. "You are not living Amish?"

"The house is wired with electricity. I use the appliances when I am here."

He took a swig of coffee, then pulled cold cuts and cheese from the refrigerator and placed them on the table, along with a loaf of whole wheat bread and plates and knives from the cabinet.

"You look hungry," he said as if to explain his actions.

She offered him a weak smile. "How does hungry look?"

"Pale and drawn, with sad eyes edged in fright."

Lizzie sipped the coffee and nodded. "I admit being frightened."

"You want to tell me what happened?"

She explained about working for Thad Thompson in hopes of learning more about his son, Andrew. Then, pausing for a moment, she pulled in a shallow breath and placed the mug on the table.

"The last time I saw Emma, she had climbed into a small motorboat with Andrew headed to the Thompsons' yacht docked in a nearby marina. Andrew had been drinking, and I tried to convince Emma not to go with him, but I couldn't dissuade her from seeing the yacht firsthand. I... I waited on the beach until the first light of dawn played over the horizon, but Emma never returned."

"I'm sorry you had to go through that."

Buoyed by the concern she saw in his gaze, she gobbled down half a sandwich and then explained about Andrew's attack this evening and her need to flee on her bike. "Here's the surprise I had stopped believing."

She took her time forming the words she knew

would take Caleb aback. "Andrew and his father said that Emma—"

She paused for a long moment.

"They said Emma is still alive."

His eyes widened ever so slightly. He pulled air through his front teeth and shook his head. "If she is alive, then where has she been all this time?"

"In one of the nursing homes Mr. Thompson owns somewhere in the Southeast. If I learn its location, I can find her."

"You probably know Thad Thompson plans to run for the senate."

She nodded. "Which is why they want Emma out of the picture."

"What?"

"From what I overheard, Andrew beat her that night and severely injured her. Since then, she has been holed up in a care facility. Now her memory is returning. If she recalls what happened, she can tell the police. Mr. Thompson doesn't want anything to ruin his chances of running for office. The easiest way to ensure she does not cause problems is to do away with her."

Caleb swallowed hard.

"Andrew said he will put an end to the problem," Lizzie continued. "Which means they plan to kill her. That's why I have to find Emma."

"You could get hurt, Lizzie. Go home to Amish Mountain."

"I can't go back knowing she's alive." She held

up her hand, palm out. "And you can't change my mind, Caleb. I'm not that young naive girl who hung around you and Emma."

"We were all friends."

"I was a third wheel as the *Englisch* say, like the adult tricycles the Amish ride here in Pinecraft. I apologize for getting in the way. If I had not been in the picture, Emma never would have gone to the beach that night."

The truth of her words cut into her anew. Lizzie had been the one who first noticed Andrew at the beach earlier in the day. Believing Caleb and Emma would soon be wed, and emboldened by her own desire to find love, Lizzie had flirted brazenly with the handsome rich boy, never realizing how her playful dalliance would end.

"Do not bring guilt upon yourself that is unwarranted, Lizzie. You didn't force Emma to sneak out that night."

"She never would have gone alone, Caleb. I knew you planned to marry. I should have been the voice of reason and stopped her from such foolishness. My father said I was to blame for her disappearance."

"Your father places Emma's wrongdoing on your shoulders, yet we both know Emma wanted more than living on a farm and raising a family. At least she thought she did."

Lizzie saw the hurt in his eyes. "She loved you, Caleb, just as you loved her. Foolish as it sounds,

Emma wanted to have fun one last time. Pinecraft is like that. A place to be carefree and dig your toes in the sand. To do things that would not be allowed at home."

He bristled. "Like sneaking out of the house to meet a young man on the beach."

"Emma did nothing wrong."

"If not, then why did you leave Amish Mountain?"

"And why did you come back to Pinecraft?" she countered. "We both have struggled with Emma's disappearance. The only way I can find peace is to find her."

Lizzie's cell rang. She dug it out of her pocket and checked the screen. "Nadine Cavanaugh. She's Mr. Thompson's full-time housekeeper."

"Don't tell her where you are," Caleb warned.

She nodded and lifted the phone to her ear. "Did you get home safely, Nadine?"

"Something's going on." The woman's voice was tight with emotion. "Security was here. They wanted to know where to find you."

Lizzie's head throbbed. "Did they tell you what happened?"

"They claimed you attacked Mr. Thompson and stole from him. I said they were looking for the wrong person. Someone else did that, not you. Then they showed me a picture from the security tape. You were running out of the house. Another picture was of the safe in Mr. Thompson's office."

"His safe?"

"They said you stole cash from the safe."

Lizzie's stomach roiled. "You've got to believe me, Nadine, I did not steal anything."

"I know you're not a thief, Elizabeth, but you are in trouble."

"I need your help. There's an envelope on Mr. Thompson's desk. It's from a nursing home."

"You want me to snoop around his office?"

"Take a picture of the return address and send it to my phone."

"I can't."

"Please, Nadine."

"They fired me, Elizabeth. Said I couldn't come back to work. I don't know what I'm gonna do this close to Christmas. I told them my husband's outta work and we've got the kids."

"I'm so sorry."

"I'm sorry too. Now I'm gonna hang up and pretend I never called you. Take care of yourself, Elizabeth. My advice is to leave town and don't ever come back."

The phone disconnected.

Lizzie dropped her cell onto the table and lowered her head into her hands. Her world was spinning out of control, and Nadine was right. She needed to get out of town before she got into more trouble.

* * *

Early the next morning, Caleb tapped on the bedroom door. "Lizzie?"

"Just a minute." Her weak response floated through the closed doorway. Water ran in the adjoining bathroom before footsteps sounded, crossing the room.

The door opened and he was taken aback by her appearance. Lizzie's hair was damp and slightly disheveled and her face drawn. Dark rings circled her eyes so that he wondered if she had slept at all. Always slender, she looked even more so this morning as if a strong wind would blow her away.

"Sorry I woke you, but there's something I want you to see."

She followed him to the kitchen table where a newspaper lay open.

He tapped the paper. "Earlier this morning, I hurried to the store to grab some pastries for breakfast and a newspaper."

Stepping closer, she peered at the newsprint. "The *Herald-Tribune*?"

"Have you been following the recent editorials?"

She shook her head. "Is there something about last night?"

"More or less." Caleb pointed to an article. "Jeb Grayson is a freelance journalist I read at times. Ever since word circulated that Mr. Thompson may run for the senate, Grayson's been posing questions about his candidacy. Most folks believe Thompson is a shoo-in. He has money and backing, only Grayson says people need to take a closer look."

"After what happened last night, I agree with the journalist."

"Today's piece mentions Thompson's adoptive son."

"Andrew?"

Caleb nodded. "Seems the kid was a problem in his high school years. According to Grayson, Thad Thompson's money got Andrew out of a lot of scrapes."

"And law enforcement gave the kid a pass?" she asked.

"Or received a little something for their lack of interest in Andrew's antics. I emailed Jeb Grayson this morning and said a friend and I wanted to talk to him about the Thompson family. I explained that we had information he might find interesting and told him to contact me."

Caleb checked his phone, then retrieved a mug from the cabinet, poured coffee and handed it to her. "Pastries are on the counter by the stove. Help yourself."

"*Danki.*"

Surprised by her response, he asked, "You're still Amish?"

She took a sip of coffee and shrugged. "I'm not

sure what I am, but one thing is certain—I won't go back to Amish Mountain until I find Emma."

"If she hadn't disappeared, things would be different."

Lizzie nodded. "You and Emma would have married. There would be children by now."

"And Eli Beiler would have courted you."

She shook her head decisively. "Eli was a nice man, but he did nothing for my heart."

"Your heart?" Caleb laughed. "Love grows in a marriage when two people have common goals, even if love is not there in the beginning."

"You have listened to old men sitting around a potbellied stove, Caleb. You should instead move to the kitchen and hear the women."

He raised his brow and glanced around. "We are in the kitchen. Tell me what the women say."

"That love holds a marriage together and must be present from the onset. Like a strong vine, it is the foundation upon which everything else grows."

"Are they not saying the same as the men?"

She smiled. "A woman wants to be loved. This is not something a man needs."

He pulled out his cell phone and chuckled. "I'll check my phone in case Grayson emailed me while you dream about love."

"I am not dreaming, Caleb. Besides, love is not for all women." She squared her shoulders.

"I made my choice and will follow my head instead of my heart."

"Your head could get you in more trouble." He stared at his phone. "Grayson emailed me."

Caleb tapped a number into his cell and raised it to his ear. The reporter answered almost immediately.

"I contacted you earlier by email," Caleb explained. "You said to call."

"If you have information about Thad Thompson, I'm interested. Can you meet me at the Chicken Shack in an hour?"

Caleb glanced at the wall clock. "We'll see you there."

He disconnected and passed the details on to Lizzie. "He wants to meet us at nine thirty."

"I know the place. The Chicken Shack is a hole in the wall that serves breakfast and lunch not far from the water."

"I'll drive."

Lizzie raised a brow as if surprised by his comment.

"The landlord leaves an old Chevy on the property that he allows me to use," Caleb explained. "It's a clunker, affectionately called the Beach Mobile."

"Even a clunker sounds good this morning. My muscles are sore from last night. Give me a few minutes to freshen up." She hurried into the guest room and closed the door behind her. Caleb swallowed down his unease.

Lizzie looked fragile. She also looked vulnerable. Could she find Emma? Or would Andrew Thompson and Estate Security find her first?

THREE

Caleb slipped a jersey over his shirt and suspenders and returned to the kitchen to wait for Lizzie. She joined him there with her face scrubbed and her hair hanging loose around her shoulders. He handed her a jacket.

"What's this for?" she asked.

"In spite of the sunshine, the air is cool today, plus the jacket will cover your clothing in case anyone is looking for one of Mr. Thompson's housekeepers."

After putting it on, she tugged at the long sleeves and laughed. "I feel like a drowned cat."

"Push the sleeves up on your arms. Even in winter, the Amish and Mennonite ladies frequently walk along the beach in their long skirts. No one will give you a second thought. But we still need to be careful."

"I called my roommate. Sally's adding a few things to a small tote I kept packed in my closet in case something like this ever happened. I'll call her back and arrange to meet after we talk to the reporter, if you don't mind driving me."

"Can you trust her?"

"Completely. She knows my background and will use care to ensure she's not being followed."

He moved to the kitchen door. "Wait here until I check the area."

Stepping outside, he peered over the fence, re-lieved that the neighborhood was quiet and empty of strange cars parked on the side of the road.

"The street looks clear." He held the door and locked it after her. "The car is parked at the rear of the property."

Lizzie raised the hood of his jacket over her head, hurried to the car and slipped into the pas-senger seat. Caleb climbed behind the wheel. Looking over his shoulder, he backed onto the street.

"Might be a good idea to keep your head down until we leave Pinecraft in case security is still hanging around."

She complied with his request. He flicked his gaze around the neighborhood and nodded to a few of the folks who biked past them.

"Not many people on the street this morning, which is good. Another few minutes and we'll be out of Pinecraft and headed to the water."

"I don't want to drive by Mr. Thompson's es-tate."

"We'll stop at the public beach. The marina is visible from there. If Andrew arrived on his father's yacht, it'll be anchored in the marina."

He checked the rearview mirror and touched her arm. "We're out of Pinecraft."

Lizzie raised upright in the seat.

"You covered a good deal of territory last night," Caleb said.

"Thanks to my bike and back roads and alleys. I knew my apartment would be the first place they would look."

"That's why I'm concerned about you meeting your roommate. She could be followed."

"I told you, Sally will be careful."

Caleb hoped Lizzie was right.

They drove in silence until the water appeared in the distance. "It is beautiful, *yah*?" Caleb said.

"I loved coming here with my family."

"Especially when the winter weather was cold on the mountain." He pulled into the parking lot and cut the engine.

A few people strolled along the water's edge, and a number of families with young children played in the sand.

Lizzie stepped out of the car and raised her hand over her eyes to ward off the sun's bright glare. "There."

She pointed to the marina. "The last yacht on the right."

Caleb whistled under his breath. "It's a beauty."

He raised his cell phone and using the camera, he zoomed in on the deck and snapped a shot and then another. "*Lady of the Seas*," he read the name painted on the vessel.

A door opened on board and a tall muscular guy with dark brown hair, wearing a white-knit fleece and khaki slacks, stepped onto the deck.

"I have a feeling Andrew Thompson just made an appearance."

Lizzie instinctively stepped back.

Caleb clicked a number of photos and then touched her arm. "Let's return to the car."

She nodded toward a large home on the water. "There's the Thompson estate."

"The camera on my phone is good. I'll zoom in and see if anything of interest appears in the shots." Caleb took a few photos of the home and grounds before they climbed into the car.

His phone rang. He raised it to his ear.

"It's Jeb." The reporter sounded anxious. "Someone's hanging around my condo. I'm not sure what's going on, but it has me worried. I can't meet where we planned. I'll contact you later."

"What if I email the information to you?"

"Yeah." Grayson snickered. "People send me a lot of things that aren't legit. Some say I'm overly cautious, but I like to meet my sources in person."

Caleb's neck twitched. "I understand. Stay safe."

"You too."

He pocketed his phone and shared what Jeb had said.

Her face blanched. "This seems to be a bigger problem than I expected."

"We'll go to the shop where I work and wait there to hear back from him. If he wants information about the Thompsons, he'll find a way to meet us."

At least, Caleb hoped he would. Bad things were underfoot, probably more than he and Lizzie realized.

"What a delightful store." Lizzie's breath caught when Caleb unlocked a side door and guided her into a small shop, adjoining one of the Pinecraft Amish marts. Framed photographs hung on the walls. Each captured a bit of Amish life.

Lizzie moved from photo to photo, enthralled with the pristine farms dotting the hillsides and stretching across the valleys. Tall silos and pastures where horses grazed sat near white farmhouses. Laundry hung on lines and flapped in the wind. Horse-drawn buggies, draft horses pulling hay wagons, flea markets and livestock auctions were all featured in earth tones, black-and-white and muted colors. The photos captured the essence of Amish life, a life she had left.

"The pictures were here when I took over the store," he explained, no doubt noting her interest in the various Amish scenes.

"This is your store?" she asked.

"I manage it. The owner lives in Cedar Key, on the Gulf Coast. I stopped there on my way south. He's a wood-carver and crafted most of the larger items."

She glanced at the baby cradles, blanket chests, small tables and knickknack shelves on display. All appeared handcrafted and intricately carved.

"The items are beautiful." She pointed to carved nameplates that hung among the photos. "Those have to be your pieces, and I'm sure you did the carving on the baby cradle and blanket chest."

"I'm also working on some larger furnishings that will be more ornately carved. I learned a lot from the owner in Cedar Key. He taught me to become a better wood-carver, as well as how to run a business."

"You were always talented, Caleb."

"My father said I was lazy. He thought a man should work the fields from sunup to sundown without spending time on other endeavors."

"Your father was wrong."

He motioned her toward the back of the shop. "We will stay in the rear office. I do not want to open the store today. If people see us through the windows, they will tap on the door and ask to enter."

Lizzie glanced again at the photos before she stepped into the back room. A computer sat on a small desk. A second table held a printer.

Caleb guided her to an easy chair in the corner. "Have a seat while I print copies of the photos of Andrew and the *Lady of the Sea*."

She settled into the chair. A leather-bound

Bible was perched on a side table. Touching the book brought back memories of sitting on benches in neighbors' homes, listening to the bishop preach, hearing the elders provide words of counsel, seeing the men on one side of the room and the women on the other, many holding infants or toddlers on their laps.

She wiggled unconsciously, remembering the hard benches and the way her back would tire about an hour or so into the service. *Mamm* said the Lord wanted Lizzie sitting up straight and being attentive, yet when she caught Emma's eye, she would be hard pressed to keep from smiling. Emma was the daring one who stretched the rules whenever possible. Like the night she had snuck out of her house to meet Andrew on the beach. If only Lizzie hadn't introduced them earlier in the day.

She pulled her hand away from the Bible and stood when Caleb neared. He held two photos in his hand.

"I blew up the pictures." He pointed to the photo of the man on the boat. "Is this Mr. Thompson's son?"

She eyed the tall man with windblown hair and an angular face. "*Yah*, that is Andrew."

Caleb held up the photograph of the vessel. "And the *Lady of the Seas* is his boat."

"His father's."

Caleb nodded. "We'll take these to show Jeb."

His phone buzzed. He lifted the cell to his ear. "*Yah?*"

Lizzie hoped they would meet the reporter soon. She was worried about what was happening at the Thompson estate and whether security was still searching for her.

"We'll see you there." Disconnecting, Caleb pointed to the door. "Jeb is meeting us at a coffee shop before he leaves town for a few days."

The drive to the small mom-and-pop shop took fifteen minutes. They parked in the rear and hurried inside through a side door. Garlands of tinsel and white lights hung from the counter, and Christmas music played softly in the background.

Lizzie slipped into a booth in the far corner while Caleb paid for two coffees and carried them to the table.

He scooted into the booth next to her. They sipped from their mugs and looked up when the door opened. A man stepped inside, medium height, stocky build, chestnut hair and scruffy beard tinged with gray. He was wearing a Florida Gators sweatshirt and jeans.

He ordered a coffee and carried it to the booth. "You folks waiting for someone?"

"Jeb Grayson?" Caleb asked.

He nodded, glanced at the door and then slipped into the seat. Caleb extended his hand and introduced himself and Lizzie.

"I don't have long," the reporter said. "Tell me what you've got?"

"Andrew Thompson," Caleb began and looked at Lizzie as if to bring her into the conversation. "We may have more information about his youthful mishaps."

Caleb drew out the photos and pointed to the picture on the man on the ship. "Is this the guy you know as Andrew Thompson?"

Jeb nodded. "That's him. But he hasn't been in the US for the last three years. Where did you take this picture?"

"At the marina near the Thompsons' house. Andrew's back in town."

Jeb studied the photo and nodded. "That's why I've been followed. It's probably Thompson's security guards making sure I don't go near the estate or their yacht. Thad Thompson is none too happy about the articles I've written." He glanced at his watch again. "What else do you have?"

Lizzie told him about Emma meeting Andrew on the beach three years ago.

"You were with her?"

"She was my best friend," Lizzie explained. "I couldn't let her go alone."

"Where were you staying at the time?"

"In Pinecraft."

"You're Amish?" he asked.

"Yes, although I haven't lived Amish for over a year."

"What happened that night?"

"Andrew asked Emma if she wanted to tour his yacht. The last I saw her, she was in a small motorboat with Andrew heading to his yacht. I waited on the beach for her, never thinking she would be gone long."

Lizzie bit her lip. "Emma never came back."

Jeb leaned closer. "Did you contact the police?"

"Just before dawn, I hurried back to the cabin where my family and I were staying. Emma's parents knocked on our door soon after that, saying they couldn't find her."

"Did you tell them where you had been?"

"I had to."

"Was law enforcement notified? I know the Amish don't usually include the police."

"Emma's father contacted the authorities. They questioned me and claimed to talk to Mr. Thompson. He said Andrew was on their island so he couldn't have been the boy on the beach."

"You and your family eventually traveled home?"

"A few days later. I couldn't get Emma off my mind." She explained about leaving the community and working her way into a housekeeping job in Thompson's mansion.

"Last night, Andrew returned home," she continued. "I overheard him tell his father that Emma was alive. She's in a long-term care facility his uncle manages."

Jeb nodded. "Thompson owns nursing homes and rehab facilities throughout the Southeast. Harold Fraser, a newspaper buddy of mine who works for the *Atlanta-Journal Constitution*, has been looking into his business practices. We keep each other informed on what we've learned. Harold believes some of Thompson's people are walking a fine line between legitimate operations and fraud, although he can't prove anything at this point."

"Won't everything come out in the open if Thompson runs for office?"

"He thinks he's above the law and probably believes he can buy his way out of any situation."

"Do you know where the uncle's nursing home is located?" Lizzie asked. "Mr. Thompson said Emma has become a problem. She's remembering what happened and the uncle is worried she'll talk."

"I don't know anything about the uncle, but I do know Mrs. Thompson's maiden name was Whitaker. Do a search of nursing homes and see if you uncover a manager with the last name of either Thompson or Whitaker."

"What about your buddy Harold?" Caleb asked. "Would he have a list of the managers' names?"

"I'll text him and let you know what he says." Jeb typed a message into his phone before glancing at his watch. "Look, I've gotta go, but there's something else you should know. Over the last three years, a few young women have gone missing on Getaway Island where Andrew's been working. My source says each of them was last seen in his company. He's a nasty drunk who likes to beat up women. Rumor has it he killed those girls. No hard evidence yet, and Daddy pays his security guards well so they turn a blind eye to some things, especially young women who get involved with his son."

Lizzie nodded. "Mr. Thompson mentioned other women. Evidently, Emma is fortunate to have survived."

"You're right about that. Andrew was less aggressive three years ago. As his drinking has increased, so have his attacks."

He glanced at the door, then back at Lizzie and Caleb.

"Watch your back," Jeb warned. "The cops here are pro-Thompson. He's vowed to increase the police pension and the officers are supporting his candidacy. This is the wrong time to come out against any of the Thompsons."

Lizzie leaned across the table. "Are you saying I shouldn't try to find Emma?"

"I'm saying be careful."

He downed the rest of his coffee and stood. A shot fired—the glass window shattered and Jeb gasped. Blood oozed from his arm.

Lizzie screamed.

"Run." Jeb pointed them toward the back door. "Through the kitchen. There's a rear exit."

"What about you?" Caleb asked.

"I'll follow you out in a minute or two." The reporter clutched his upper arm. "Go now so you can get a head start. Hurry."

Caleb grabbed Lizzie. They raced through the kitchen to the car and exited the parking area by way of the alley.

She glanced back. Another round of gunfire erupted. Her heart pounded.

"Are they following us?" Caleb glanced in the rearview mirror.

"I don't see anyone."

He accelerated and turned north at the intersection. "We'll take the long route back to Pinecraft."

"Will we be safe there?"

"I'm not sure you'll be safe anywhere in the city. Like Jeb said, you need to get away before they catch you."

And if they caught her, what would happen then?

She was afraid to voice the question aloud for fear of what Caleb might say. People were after her, a man who was investigating Mr. Thompson had been shot and she was accused of stealing from the millionaire.

Caleb's phone rang. He checked the monitor. "It's Jeb."

After accepting the call, he hit Speaker. "Are you okay?"

"A flesh wound. I heard back from my pal in Atlanta."

"Harold Fraser? The guy who works for the *AJC*?"

"That's right. Warren Whitaker runs Respite Haven. It's located northeast of Freemont, Georgia. A small town off the beaten path."

"My aunt and uncle own a farm in that part of the state."

"Tell Lizzie to get out of Sarasota for her own safety. I'm leaving in about an hour. Keep in touch and let me know when you locate Emma."

"Will do."

"How can I get to Freemont?" Lizzie asked once the call disconnected.

"An Amish tour bus leaves Pinecraft for Indiana later today. It stops near Freemont."

"Then I need to be on that bus."

"I'll call the travel company and reserve two seats," Caleb said.

"Two seats?"

"*Yah*." Caleb nodded. "I'm going with you."

FOUR

Caleb couldn't let Lizzie travel to Freemont alone. He would never forgive himself if something happened to her, and after the shooting at the coffee shop, her situation had gone from dangerous to deadly. Although the shots had been meant for Jeb, Lizzie could have been injured. Thankfully, the reporter's wound was superficial, not that a flesh wound wasn't significant.

Jeb had been vocal about his distrust of Thad Thompson, and someone had retaliated with gunfire. Caleb would like to think the shots had been meant to warn Jeb that he was delving into something that was better left unsaid—or at least not exposed in print. Was Estate Security the culprit, or was someone else working as Mr. Thompson's secret police?

Lizzie glanced at the road behind them.

"No one's following us," he assured her.

"Traffic is heavy, Caleb. How can you be certain we're not being followed?"

"I don't see any law-enforcement vehicles or Estate Security." He glanced at the nearby cars. "Everyone around us seems intent on getting to their destinations, which is good for us."

"I should feel reassured. At least somewhat. While you keep your eyes on the other cars, I'll call my roommate." Lizzie pulled out her phone and hit the contact number.

Caleb could hear the faint ring of the phone.

"Sally?" Lizzie said in lieu of a greeting. "I'm okay. Really."

She glanced at Caleb. "The laundromat? Let me check."

Pulling the phone from her ear, she asked, "Can you drive me to Suds Laundromat? It's located about three miles from my apartment?" She provided the address.

"I don't think that's wise, Lizzie. The cops and security could follow Sally. Your safety is more important than some favorite items of clothing"

"Please, Caleb."

He hesitated a moment, then seeing the intensity of her gaze, he nodded. "Okay. I'll turn at the next intersection. We should be there in fifteen minutes."

She relayed the information. "Be careful, Sally. If you don't feel safe or if you notice strange people milling around, we can cancel the meeting. Otherwise, I'll enter through the rear door. You found the bag in the closet, right?"

Lizzie smiled. "Great. Thanks. See you in a few minutes."

She disconnected. "I know you're worried, Caleb, but if security or the police are watching the apartment, it's doubtful they would be concerned about a woman lugging a laundry basket to her car."

"I hope you're right."

He hadn't thought Lizzie would be in danger at the coffee shop, yet she could have been wounded or worse. At the moment, he was worried about her safety. The sooner she left Sarasota, the better.

"There!" Lizzie pointed to the laundromat situated in the middle of a strip mall. She glanced at the clock on the console. "Sally should be there by now. If you circle to the rear of the building, I can enter through the back door."

"First we need to check the parking lot."

He drove past the front of the shops, then circled to the rear and braked to a stop at the back door.

"Get your tote from Sally and hurry back to the car," Caleb cautioned. "Remember, the less she knows, the better for her and for you. Don't mention where you're going or that you know anything about Emma's whereabouts."

"I trust her, Caleb."

"But pressure could be put on her to reveal what she knows."

Lizzie's pulse kicked up a notch. She glanced over her shoulder, then shoved open the car door and raced inside. She spied Sally standing near one of the washing machines.

"I've been worried about you," her roommate said as the two women embraced.

"This might be a good time to visit that friend of yours from high school," Lizzie suggested.

"Janet Dean?"

Lizzie nodded. "Stay with her for a few days until everything cools down."

"Do you think that's necessary?"

Lizzie glanced at the other people in the laundromat—a twenty-something reading a magazine, a woman holding a toddler on her lap and a middle-aged man transferring clothing from a washer to a dryer—and nodded. "You could be in danger."

"You're worrying me."

She grabbed the tote and hugged her roommate. "Take care of yourself, Sally."

As she turned toward the rear door, two men dressed in khaki slacks and navy polos entered from the front.

Her heart lodged in her throat.

Sally followed Lizzie's gaze. "That's them, isn't it?"

Lizzie nodded, then squeezed Sally's hand. "Stay safe."

She hurried to the rear door and glanced back. The men caught sight of her and raced forward. Sally lifted a basket of laundry off one of the machines and pretended to trip. Clothing spilled onto the floor.

"Sorry," she said, blocking their path.

"Move it, lady."

Lizzie raced outside. Her heart nearly stopped. Caleb was nowhere to be seen.

One of the guards slammed through the door. She took off running, her heart pounding in time with her footfalls.

At the corner, she turned left and spied a fast-food restaurant. She pushed through the door and headed to the rear of the eatery, all the while keeping her gaze on the road.

She slipped into a booth and hunched down.

The man who had chased after her ran past on the sidewalk. She let out the breath she was holding. Although relieved, she knew he would double back and return to the laundromat. She had to find Caleb before the man found her.

Where was Lizzie?

Caleb heart pounded like a jackhammer. When she had hurried inside, he had parked in a side alley where his car was out of sight but he could see the rear door of the laundromat.

How had he missed her? His pulse raced with his mind thinking all sorts of scenarios and none of them good.

A dark sedan circled the lot, making his stomach sour and his head ache with thoughts of what Lizzie might have to endure at the hands of Thad Thompson and his son.

The sedan turned onto the main road. With no other vehicles in sight, Caleb left his car, raced across the parking lot and entered the laundromat. A woman stood at the front window, hugging her arms. She looked about Lizzie's age, and from her body language, he knew she was scared.

"Excuse me, ma'am," he said as he approached her. "Did you see a pretty brown-haired lady in here a few minutes ago?"

The woman stared briefly at him as if trying to decide if he were friend or foe. "Are you Lizzie's friend?" she finally asked.

"Where is she?"

"I… I don't know. She left through the back door. I tried to block the men, but one ran after her. The other one raced out the front. He jumped into a car and circled the lot before he picked up his buddy and drove away."

"You saw them leave the area?" he asked.

Sally nodded. "But I'm worried about Lizzie."

So was Caleb. He retraced his steps back to his car and flicked his gaze over the parking area.

His phone rang. He pulled it to his ear. "Yeah?"

"Caleb, where are you?"

Lizzie's voice. He exhaled the breath he had been holding. "In an alley behind the laundromat. Are you all right?"

"Wait there. I'll find you."

"Lizzie—" But she had already disconnected. His heart pounded so hard he thought it might explode. He started the engine and kept his gaze on the laundromat.

Would Lizzie find him? Or was security still in the area, and would they find her first?

FIVE

Lizzie's heart raced as she peered from the fast-food restaurant and eyed the street, searching for the security sedan. Traffic was light, and once assured the guards were nowhere in sight, she pulled the door open, stepped outside and hurried around the corner.

She glanced over her shoulder to be certain no one was following her and then ran to the end of the alley where Caleb was parked. She slipped into the passenger's side and grabbed his arm. "I couldn't find you."

He stepped on the accelerator. "We need to get out of here."

She dropped the tote at her feet.

"You got your stuff?" he asked.

"I did, but I'm worried about Sally. Did you see her?"

"We met when I went inside to find you. She said the security sedan had pulled out of the lot."

Relief swept over Lizzie. "I was more worried about her safety than my own. I'll call and make certain she got away without any problems."

Sally answered on the second ring and quickly said, "Are you okay, Lizzie?"

"That's what I wanted to ask you."

"I tried to stop the men, but they were determined to catch you. A tall handsome guy came into the laundromat some minutes after the security guys drove away. He was worried about you."

"That's Caleb." She glanced at him and smiled.

"He's a keeper, Lizzie. I don't know what your relationship is, but if there's anything going on, I say stay with him. The look on his face told me how he feels about you. I'd do anything to have a guy like that on my side."

Lizzie heart fluttered. She could feel heat rise in her cheeks. "You always were a romantic."

Sally laughed. "I know what I saw in his expression."

Except Caleb was spoken for, and the woman he loved was who they were hoping to find.

"I'll call you when all this is over," Lizzie said.

"Expect prayers. Take care of yourself, dear friend."

"The rent this month—"

"Don't worry about it. I'll be in touch."

She disconnected.

"Wise choice not to tell Sally where we're going," he said as she pocketed her phone.

"Just following your instructions."

"You make me sound like I'm ordering you around."

"You would never do that." Which was one of the reasons she liked him.

They had been brought together again because of Emma and because Lizzie had needed someplace to hide. The three of them had grown up together, but Caleb always seemed to pair up with Emma.

Or had Emma paired up with Caleb?

She regularly had her eyes on handsome guys and Caleb certainly was that.

Lizzie's heart went out to him. It must have been hard to lose someone just before he planned to ask for her hand in marriage.

"Look, Caleb, I've pulled you into something you may not be one hundred percent behind. You don't need to go with me."

"Oh, Lizzie." He let out an exasperated breath. "You think you can do it all. Let me help you, okay?"

"I don't want you doing something that goes against your better judgment."

"How could I turn my back on Emma?"

Lizzie nodded, feeling overcome with a sadness she didn't expect. *Gott* had drawn her back to Caleb, but not for her own need. They had been paired together again to find Emma.

Her friend and Caleb's wife-to-be.

If only the realization wasn't so hard to accept.

"You can wait at my studio," Caleb said as they neared Pinecraft. "Stay in the office area and don't go into the main shop even if someone taps on the door."

"I'll be careful," Lizzie said with a nod.

"The first thing I need to do is return my landlord's car. He's been gracious enough to let me use it around town, but the engine needs some work and driving it a long distance could be a problem. Plus, I don't want to abuse his thoughtfulness."

"So we'll bus north?" she asked.

He nodded. "Taking the chartered bus that leaves from Pinecraft is the safest option. Two buses arrived yesterday and dropped off passengers. One of the buses is making the return trip this morning. The second one will leave later in the day. Most of the passengers traveling north will be Amish or Mennonite. We'll need to dress as if we're Amish to blend in with the other folks."

"You mean wear plain clothing?"

"I'll try to find a dress and *kapp* for you. There is a thrift store. Sometimes Amish clothing is offered for sale."

"That's not necessary." She pointed to her tote. "I have the dress I wore when I left Willkommen in my bag, along with my *kapp* and a cape and bonnet."

"You can change clothes while you're at my shop. I'll make our reservations and pick up a few things at the cottage."

He drove into Pinecraft, parked in the rear of his shop and ushered her inside. "You'll be safe here. Just stay in the office."

"How long before you come back?" she asked.

"As soon as possible."

Her eyes were wide with worry.

"Everything is going to be okay, Lizzie. We'll get out of town today. Security won't find you."

He didn't want to leave her, but he needed to return the car to his landlord and pack a small bag for the trip. How long would it take to find Emma? A day or two. Not more.

Once they found her, she and Lizzie would go home to Amish Mountain and Caleb would return to Pinecraft. Coming back to the cottage alone would be difficult. He had been with Lizzie for less than twenty-four hours, but she had already gotten under his skin. In a good way.

A very good way.

When the door closed behind Caleb, Lizzie felt overcome with sadness and very much alone. She stared at the tidy office and the photos on the wall. A few shots were of Amish farms at sunrise. She could see the dew on the ground and the leaves in beautiful shades of autumn. The quiet landscape whispered of home and community and everything she loved about the mountain she had left.

She thought back to her youth, to the summer fun and times together after chores were done. She would run down the mountain to where Emma lived. Together, they would hurry to the river. Caleb would meet them there with his fishing rod, and together, they would enjoy the afternoon until it was time to return home to help with the evening meal.

The memory of laughter and sunshine and the warmth of friendship surrounded her. For the last three years, she had not only missed Emma, she had also missed Caleb and the bond they had shared during their youth.

Taking in a deep breath, she unzipped her tote and stared at the clothing she had worn the day she left home. A lump filled her throat. She pulled the dress free and shook it, grateful for good fabric that resisted wrinkles. Flicking her gaze around the room to ensure her privacy, she slipped out of her housekeeping uniform and donned the Amish dress. Both blue but both so different.

She retrieved the small box of straight pins in the bottom of the tote and secured the dress as she had done for so many years. Why had she left home?

Because of Emma? Or was there another reason? Perhaps because of her father. He was proud of his sons, but how did he feel about his only daughter? Lizzie was someone who helped *Mamm* in the kitchen and prepared food for the men and sewed their breaches and shirts and waistcoats.

That's why she never wanted to marry. She did not want to be someone's domestic servant. If she married, she wanted to be a wife and a partner.

And Caleb? Her heart warmed. He had always thought of her as an equal, a friend. If only she could find someone like him, then perhaps she would say yes to marriage.

Gott knew she loved children and wanted a family, but she did not want to live life under the beck and call of a domineering husband. Scripture said equally yoked, yet the marriages she saw were too heavily weighted for the man. Not the woman.

With a shrug, she pulled her hair into a bun and drew her prayer *kapp* from the tote. Amish women covered their hair when they prayed. Wearing their *kapps* at all times ensured they were always ready to pray.

Had she been faithful to prayer since she had left home? She shook her head, ashamed that she had ignored *Gott* and thought of her own need to find her friend. Everything had been about her, which was not the Amish way.

She hesitated for a long moment before placing the *kapp* on her head. For some reason, she had expected it to be heavy, like a burden. Instead, the starched fabric was light as air, and she felt a sense of well-being as she settled it on her head.

How could she explain the feeling? A coming home of sorts, yet she was still in Caleb's office.

She would have laughed, if the situation were not so dire. Security was searching for her. She needed to leave Pinecraft today so the thugs Mr. Thompson had hired would not find her.

She glanced at the wall clock. How long had Caleb been gone? Surely only half an hour or so, yet in that period of time, she had gone from being an *Englischer* back to her Amish roots. That journey had been significant in the big scheme of things, yet she worried about the future. She wanted to be anyplace, except in Pinecraft where people were searching for her.

She always thought she could do everything by herself, but at the moment, she needed Caleb's support and encouragement.

Lizzie glanced again at the wall clock.

She needed Caleb. She needed him now.

SIX

Nothing looked out of order when Caleb parked the car in the back of his rental house. He hurried inside, packed a few things in a small bag, grabbed his black hat and traded his jersey for his Amish waistcoat and suspenders. A car ambled along the road in front of the cottage. Two men he didn't recognize sat in the front seat.

Englischers interested in the Amish frequently drove through Pinecraft, but the men weren't tourists. He made note of the car, a dark sedan with Florida plates. A long scratch was etched on the driver's door as if the car had been keyed. The windows were tinted so he couldn't see the men's faces, but instinctively he knew they were trouble.

He waited until the car had passed and then hurried to his shop and tapped lightly on the side door.

"Lizzie, it's Caleb."

He unlocked the door and stepped inside. She was standing in the middle of the office, wearing a calf-length blue dress with her dark hair drawn into a bun. His chest tightened and he pulled in a breath.

She smoothed her fingers over the skirt and looked at him with wide eyes and raised brows. "I was worried you might not return for me."

How could she think that?

"A strange car drove past the cottage. I waited until it was out of sight." He glanced at the wall clock. "We need to leave."

"What about the bus?"

"It should be pulling into the parking lot now."

"And your store?" she asked.

"Remaining closed for a few days is not a problem."

She grabbed her tote. "Then I'm ready."

Caleb nodded. "Walk at a normal pace. Keep your eyes down and don't look surprised or frightened."

"Easier said than done, as the *Englischers* say."

He opened the door. "I'll go first."

After checking the back lot and searching for a sedan with dark windows, he motioned her forward. "The way is clear."

She searched the area just as he had done before she stepped outside. He locked the door and pointed to the far side of the building. "We're not going far. The bus will stop at the tourist church. We need to get there as soon as we can."

"I appreciate you going with me, Caleb."

"As independent as you have always been, Lizzie, I am sure you would have been fine without me, but it is good to be together. Plus, we will visit my aunt and uncle. They will provide a place for us to stay."

"Your mother's sister?"

He nodded. "Aunt Martha is a *gut* woman. Her

husband, Zach, works hard, although they have no children."

"I'm sorry."

"Martha says it is *Gott*'s will, yet I know it is hard for both of them. Uncle Zach could use help on his farm. One man working alone." Caleb shrugged. "Martha does what she can, but she has also the house and cooking to occupy her time."

"I will enjoy meeting your aunt, especially if she is anything like your mother."

He smiled. "My mother always liked you."

"Me?" Lizzie looked surprised and stared at him for a long moment.

A car turned the corner near them. A dark sedan with tinted windows.

He touched her arm. "We must hurry."

"Who's in the car?" Lizzie's face was tight.

"I'm not sure." Caleb glanced back, relieved that the vehicle continued on.

He must have let out a stiff breath because Lizzie turned to him. "Do you think they're Estate Security?"

"I don't know. We will take a short detour to the bus station in case the car drives this way again." He checked his watch. "We have a few extra minutes."

An Amish man with a potbelly and a graying beard passed them by on an adult tricycle popular in the area. Caleb raised his hand in greeting, then placed his hand on Lizzie's back and hurried her along the road.

Clouds rolled in overhead and a cool breeze blew from the west. "I can carry your bag if it is heavy."

"It is fine, but thank you, Caleb, for the offer."

Another sedan appeared. His heart quickened as he spied the scratch on the side of the vehicle.

Lizzie grabbed his arm. "It is the same car as earlier."

"Your bonnet will hide your face. Remember, they are looking for Mr. Thompson's housekeeper and not an Amish woman."

He pointed ahead to the church parking area. "The bus has arrived."

A number of people—some Amish, others Mennonite—were waiting. Friends and family members gathered around them to say goodbye.

Caleb thought of his own family three years ago. Emma had been the first to greet him when they arrived. Two weeks later, her absence had hung like a pall over their departure.

He hated to think that she had been held against her will. All this time, he had vacillated between believing she had run off with another man—or had been killed. Shame on him for such thoughts, but Emma had been as flighty as a hummingbird, never content with her lot in life. She was always looking for something new.

A group of Amish families milled around the

parking lot. Many rolled suitcases behind them. Other folks waited for the driver to load their luggage in the bottom of the bus.

"Stand in that group of people near the bus and act like you know them while I talk to the driver and confirm our reservations."

He watched Lizzie enter the crowd. She glanced back at him as if seeking his approval. He nodded and smiled weakly, then studied the surrounding area and searched for the keyed car and the men wearing Estate Security uniforms.

Satisfied the guards were not nearby, he headed to where the driver stood, chatting with a number of Amish men. The group was jovial and the driver seemed to enjoy the comradery.

At long last, he stepped away from the group and approached Caleb. The driver confirmed their reservations and then began loading luggage. Passengers started to board.

Caleb hurried back to where he had left Lizzie. His heart raced. He did not see her.

They should have stayed together. What had he been thinking? He wasn't thinking of Lizzie's safety.

He had to find her. Now.

Lizzie huddled behind a small building at the side of the church and kept her eyes on the two men in Estate Security uniforms.

Trying to escape on a tour bus from Pinecraft

was too risky. She should have asked Caleb to drive her to a neighboring town where she could have boarded a bus far from Mr. Thompson's men. As it was, she felt completely exposed and worried she stood out from the crowd.

She had lived in the *Englisch* world since she left Amish Mountain and feared those months away from her faith had changed her so she could easily be spotted as a fake—a fake Amish woman who tried to walk in both worlds and did not succeed in either.

Here she was hiding from two men who were intent on capturing her. No telling what Mr. Thompson or his son, Andrew, would do with her, including taking her aboard their luxury yacht and sailing to Getaway Island where, if what Jeb said was true, women had a history of disappearing.

She shivered and pulled her cape across her chest.

Glancing toward the bus, she spied Caleb.

She needed to get his attention, but in so doing, she would alert the security men who stood on the far side of the park. One of them retrieved a cell phone from his pocket and raised it to his ear. He peered around the park and said something into his phone. With a definite nod of his head, he tapped his buddy's shoulder, said something to him and then spoke into the phone again before he returned the mobile device to his pocket.

The two men hurried to where their vehicle was parked. At that moment, a convertible sports car with the top down pulled to a stop beside their sedan. Her heart nearly stopped as she recognized the man behind the wheel. Andrew Thompson.

He spoke to the security guards, then pointed to the nearby east–west thoroughfare and motioned west toward the Gulf. The men nodded before they climbed into their sedan and followed him out of Pinecraft.

Lizzie felt like a helium balloon that had deflated as she watched the two cars turn west onto Bahia Vista Street and disappear from sight. Sighing with relief, she stepped from her hiding spot.

Caleb hurried toward her. "I could not find you."

He didn't have to tell her what he was thinking. The strain on his face said enough.

"The guards are persistent, Caleb. I saw you looking for me, but I didn't want to alert their notice. One of them received a phone call, then Andrew Thompson appeared in a sports car with the top down. They left Pinecraft a minute or two later and turned toward the Gulf."

"Let's get on board the bus in case they return."

Lizzie glanced at the other passengers as she climbed onto the bus and headed to a pair of seats near the rear exit. In her youth, Lizzie had anticipated her family's trips to Florida, although going home always came with a bit of sadness, knowing their Pinecraft vacation was over. Since Emma's disappearance, the Florida vacation spot brought back too many images Lizzie wanted to wipe from her memory.

Caleb placed their bags on the overhead ledge and slipped into the seat next to her. Their arms touched. All too aware of his muscular biceps and wide shoulders, she instinctively moved closer to the window.

"Do you have enough room?" he asked.

She nodded curtly and wrapped her skirt around her legs. "I am fine."

"You're trembling," he said.

"Only a little."

The near run-in with the security guards and seeing Andrew Thompson again were reasons enough for her trembling, but sitting so close to Caleb unsettled her even more. As much as she tried to ignore her feelings, he had always had a place in her heart.

Lizzie looked back at the Amish vacation community and many of the landmark buildings that had been so special to her in her youth. Now she saw the area as a place of danger.

Relieved to be leaving Pinecraft, she was worried about the journey ahead. Would they find Emma in a nursing home near Freemont? Lizzie hoped she would. Finding Emma was Lizzie's first priority.

SEVEN

"*D*id you have a *gut* vacation?" an Amish man sitting across the aisle from Caleb asked. He was tall and slender with a plump wife and three adorable children.

"Pinecraft is always a relaxing spot," Caleb replied, then turned back to Lizzie, hoping to deflect the man's attention.

"We usually go after the New Year," the man continued. "We are visiting family at that time this year and decided to go after harvest but before Christmas."

"A wise decision," Caleb said. "The weather has been pleasant. Warm days, cool nights."

His wife opened a tin of cookies and passed them to Caleb. "You would like something sweet, *yah*? The trip goes faster when the belly is full."

"Thank you." He accepted the offered tin, selected a large cookie and held the tin out for Lizzie.

She took a cookie for herself. "*Danki.*"

"Where do you folks live?" the Amish man asked when Caleb handed back the tin.

"We're from Willkommen."

"In the mountains, *yah*?"

"Have you been there?"

The man shook his head. "But I have a friend

who moved there. Levi Miller. Do you know of him perchance?"

"I know John Miller and his father, Matt Miller, but not Levi."

"Yet it is a small world, so I thought I would ask. We are from Shipshewana."

"Indiana is a beautiful state," Caleb said.

"With cold winters, which is why we enjoy our time in Florida."

The man's wife tugged on her husband's arm. "Let the young people have time for themselves, David."

He chuckled. "My wife thinks I am too forward."

"No problem, sir." Caleb took the man's comment as a way to disconnect from the conversation. David was friendly but inquisitive, and Caleb didn't want to fend off difficult questions that could place either Lizzie or himself in jeopardy.

"How long until we get to Freemont?" Lizzie asked.

"We should cross the state line mid-afternoon. From there, we will drive another few hours or so."

"Are you sure your aunt and uncle will have room for me?" she asked.

"I am sure. They will be happy to have company. You will like them," he added to reassure her.

And they would like her.

How could anyone not like Lizzie? He glanced out the side window and then turned his gaze to her as she watched the countryside pass by. She had matured over the last three years, and although her concern for Emma dampened some of the enthusiasm he remembered from their youth, Lizzie's beauty had grown more pronounced. Her pretty face and flashing eyes drew him in, along with her smile that warmed him to the core. In addition to her outer beauty, he also admired her determination and commitment to finding Emma. Lizzie was a true friend with a huge heart.

Yah, he thought, his aunt and uncle would recognize her inner goodness and, like him, would be drawn to their unexpected houseguest.

He and Lizzie both settled back in their seats as the bus continued north. Eventually, Caleb spied the exit for Cedar Key. The state line would not be far. Out of the corner of his eye, he noticed a dark sedan with tinted windows.

The cookie he had eaten settled like a hard ball in the pit of his stomach. He flicked his gaze to the rear again and let out a sigh of relief as the car turned off the road. His mind was playing tricks on him, no doubt. He needed to relax. But with Lizzie's safety in question, relaxing was the last thing he could manage.

Lizzie's insides felt as tight as a quilt on a stretching rack. She kept thinking of Emma and what she had endured over the last three years. She also felt responsible for her friend's disappearance.

If only—

She shook her head, not ready to delve into *what-ifs*. Not today and not with Caleb sitting so close to her. The day was clear and sunny, and she felt the warmth from his body flood over her like a soft blanket.

His hand brushed hers as he pointed to a flock of white gulls that had come to rest on a farmer's pasture, sending a jolt of sensation along her arm. A tingling climbed her neck and made her pull in a tiny breath. She hadn't slept well the night before and she was tired and worried, all of which, probably, added to the mix of emotions that were playing havoc with her inner calm.

Caleb was a friend and nothing more. Although at the moment, surrounded by the Amish and Mennonite families on the bus, she longed for a different kind of relationship. She gripped her hands together in an attempt to focus on something other than the all too handsome man sitting next to her.

He glanced at her and raised his brow. "Is there a problem?"

Searching for a non-threatening way to explain her feelings, she finally said, "I am anxious about what we will find in Freemont."

"We will take this one step at a time, Lizzie,

and not move too quickly. Once we learn more about the nursing home, we will know how to proceed."

"Suppose Emma does not remember us?"

"As I said, we will take each step as it comes."

"I never should have left Pinecraft three years ago. If I had stayed, perhaps I could have found Emma sooner."

"You were seventeen. Your father expected you to go home. Could you have countered his wishes?"

Up until then, Lizzie had never gone against her father's wishes about anything. Even when she talked to the police about Emma meeting Andrew at the beach. *Datt* had told her what to say—and what to withhold. He forbid her from mentioning that she had been the first to talk to Andrew Thompson earlier in the day. An action she still regretted. Later, her *datt* had chastised her for accompanying Emma to the beach that night and insisted Lizzie was to blame for the terrible mistake both girls had made.

She sighed. "What you say is true, Caleb. My father would not allow me to counter his desires. Plus, any time I struggled with my father's demands, he became upset with me and with my mother, as well. I have always thought he had a hard time dealing with women."

Caleb touched her arm. "The woman is the

heart of the family. Is there a reason his own heart has hardened over the years?"

She shook her head. "My mother shared some of his past when I was older and struggling with the lack of love he showed to both of us. She said his father had been physically abusive and his mother had run away from her husband, leaving my father behind. He never trusted women because of being abandoned."

"Yet your mother married him."

"They were young. I do not think he was as set in his ways at that time. Perhaps having a daughter as a first child increased his upset."

"I am sorry, Lizzie."

"It is life, *yah*? We are given a family and parents that we do not choose. Our responsibility is to do our best wherever *Gott* places us."

"If your *datt* is so demanding, how did you leave home when you came to Pinecraft?"

"He wanted me to marry."

"Levi Beiler?"

She shook her head. "He found an older man who had lost his wife. He was not the man I wanted to wed."

"So you left home?"

"I had a job waitressing at a coffee shop in town. My father kept my paycheck, but I saved the tips. My mother gave me a little cash, as well. Once I had enough money, I took the bus to Pinecraft."

"You were brave."

"Perhaps foolish when I think of what could have happened. I learned of a shelter that provided short-term room and board. I worked for a cleaning team, eventually met Sally and moved in with her. I focused on the upscale homes near the water and landed a job at the cleaning service that Mr. Thompson used."

"And your father did not come after you?"

"More likely he said good riddance."

"I do not think that is the case, Lizzie, but I am sorry for the pain you had to bear."

"What about you, Caleb? Long ago, you mentioned your father did not want you to carve wood."

"He thought I was making graven images, although they were small animals that children enjoyed or that *Englischers* would place in their homes. Frogs, turtles and rabbits were favorites with the children. Now, I manage the shop, which my father would not approve of, and whittle when I have free time."

"You are talented."

"*Gott* planted the desire in my heart, but my father did not think *Gott* was involved. I struggled with his mindset. He wanted me to farm the land and forget my craft, but a part of me died when I could not work with the wood. Like you, I left home by bus and stayed with my aunt and uncle for a few weeks."

"I'm glad your relatives took you in."

"My next stop was Cedar Key, on the Gulf Coast. That's where I worked with the wood-carver." Caleb smiled sheepishly. "He said I had a good eye for the wood."

"An eye for beauty," Lizzie said with a nod.

"An eye for that which my father would not approve."

"Sometimes we must do what is necessary, even if our parents do not approve."

Lizzie glanced out the window and nudged Caleb. "That car looks familiar."

A dark sedan with tinted windows.

"I saw a similar car earlier. It turned off the road a few hours ago."

"Could it be from Sarasota?"

"It's doubtful this far north. Besides, Estate Security usually has a logo on the side of their vehicles. This car does not bear that signage."

Caleb did not seem worried, but Lizzie was. Signage or not, she feared the guards might have followed them.

Her stomach tightened. She needed to be free from them in order to find Emma.

EIGHT

Caleb saw the worry in Lizzie's eyes. "It seems something is troubling you."

"I'm concerned about the car that's following us. Is there any way the guards would know we are on the bus?"

"I don't see how, unless—" He patted his jacket and groaned.

"What?"

"I just realized my cell phone could have been pinging and sending a signal they could follow."

"Wouldn't they need access to your phone number?"

"It's on the store's website," Caleb admitted. "What about your phone, Lizzie? Is it turned on?"

"Unfortunately yes." She pulled her phone from her tote and handed it to Caleb.

"I'll take care of both mobile devices at the next stop."

Soon after they passed the state line, the intercom activated and the driver's voice filled the bus. "Folks, we'll be taking a comfort stop in about five minutes. Stretch your legs. Grab a cup of coffee. Use the facilities. Be back on the bus in thirty minutes."

They both glanced at the car that continued to follow them.

"When we get out," Caleb said, "take your tote bag with you."

"We're not returning to the bus?"

"I'm not sure. Get off quickly and head toward the ladies' restroom. I'll check out the area and meet you outside the facilities."

The bus moved into the right lane, stopped at the end of the exit ramp and turned into a large truck stop.

Caleb glanced back. His heart thudded when he realized the car had followed the bus into the gas station.

"Remember, I'll meet you outside the ladies' room."

The bus stopped. They grabbed their totes and headed for the rear door when it opened.

"Careful. The stairs are steep."

She stepped off the bus just as two men wearing khaki pants and navy shirts approached the bus driver.

"Go around the back of the bus," Caleb prompted.

Lizzie did as he instructed. He followed after her and hurried her inside the station.

"There's the restroom." He pointed to the far corner. "I'll meet up with you in a few minutes."

Caleb glanced back. The security guards were standing by the driver and watching the passengers exit the bus. Some of the older people were slow getting off, which would give Caleb more time to come up with a plan.

He hustled outside through a back door and studied the surrounding farmland. In the near distance, he saw an Amish buggy and heard the clip-clop of the horse's hooves on the pavement.

The driver—a young Amish man—turned his buggy into the station, tethered his horse to the hitching rail, then walked briskly toward the convenience store.

"Excuse me, sir." Caleb stepped in front of him. "I need your help."

Lizzie washed her hands and splashed water on her face to cool her cheeks. She peered through the restroom doorway, hoping to see Caleb. What was he doing?

She had seen the security uniforms and knew Estate Security had followed them. Would they continue to hunt her down no matter where she went?

"You are not well?" The Amish lady who had offered them cookies on the bus touched her arm.

Lizzie smiled, trying to make light of the situation. "A bit of motion sickness."

"*Ack.* This is not *gut.* I have ginger lozenges. Perhaps they would help." The woman dug in her bag, retrieved a pack of lozenges and handed them to Lizzie. "Please, try these."

"Just one. *Danki.*"

Lizzie placed the mint in her mouth and nodded her thanks.

"Shall I tell the young man you are traveling with you are not well?"

"It is not necessary, but again, I am grateful for your thoughtfulness."

"A drink of water might help, *yah*?"

Lizzie nodded. "*Yah*." Although nothing would help except getting away from the security guards.

"I will see you on the bus," the woman said as she pushed through the door.

Lizzie peered into the empty hallway. One of the security men came into view. Her heart thudded as the door swung closed.

Another woman entered and Lizzie peered out again. The security man was gone. In his place, she saw Caleb.

He motioned her forward. "The guards are outside, near the bus. We'll leave through the back door."

"But—"

"Trust me, Lizzie."

She had to trust Caleb, although at the moment, she feared being hauled back to Sarasota or to a nursing home in Georgia. Terrible things happened to young women who got involved with Andrew Thompson. She didn't want to be one of his victims. Most of all, she didn't want to end up dead.

NINE

"We must hurry." Caleb grabbed her arm and ushered her away from where the bus was parked. She longed to know where they were going, but Caleb did not have time for questions.

Had they really been tracked through their cell phones? If so, how would they ever be able to escape? The guards would have some other type of technology to trace them that Lizzie had never heard of before.

She wanted to cry, but she didn't have time for such a luxury and doing so would not help anyone.

"Hurry," Caleb said again, pointing to the far side of the station.

As they rounded the corner, she saw a buggy and an Amish man standing nearby.

He waved them forward. "It is time to leave, *yah*?"

"Thanks, Samuel." Caleb hurriedly introduced Lizzie as he helped her into the buggy. "Climb into the rear."

She complied with his instruction and tucked her tote under the seat. "How do you know Samuel?" she asked, her voice low, when Caleb hunkered down next to her.

"I saw him drive into the gas station. He needed

to use the pay phone. I told him we needed transportation."

"You hired a complete stranger to drive us to Freemont?"

"Not that far. He lives about a thirty-minute ride from here. An *Englisch* neighbor of his drives an Amish taxi. Samuel feels sure the neighbor will take us to my relatives' house."

"What will happen when the bus driver realizes we are not on the bus?"

"I told David you had motion sickness and needed to rest. A second bus is heading this way later today. I explained that if you felt better, we would take that bus. The driver may never realize we are missing, but if he questions our whereabouts, David will explain what happened."

"And our phones?"

"David is taking them to Indiana. He'll dispose of them there."

She knew Caleb was trying to lighten her anxiety, but Estate Security would not give up their search.

Samuel climbed into the front of the buggy. He flicked the reins and the mare trotted onto the main road.

Lizzie glanced through the small opening in the rear of the buggy. The bus was still parked at the station and their phones were on board. How soon before the security guards realized they had been tricked?

She never thought her quest to find Emma would make her become the hunted. Her father was right. Lizzie was impulsive and too often acted without thinking of the consequences. Not only was she in danger but Caleb was, as well.

Caleb felt like a trapped mouse in a cage. Grateful though he was for the ride, sitting hunched over in the rear of Samuel's buggy was uncomfortable. Lizzie's face showed the wear that the stress was taking. She said nothing, but he knew she was frightened. It had been his idea to take the bus to Freemont. He never thought his cell phone would serve as a tracking mechanism. Foolish of him. He should have used his head.

Now that the security guards had followed them into Georgia, Caleb doubted they would give up the search until they had more information to provide Mr. Thompson.

He glanced out the rear of the buggy.

"The bus is approaching," he said to alert Samuel.

"We will turn off the main road just ahead. The back roads will be a safer ride for the buggy."

The turnoff could not come soon enough for Caleb.

Lizzie grabbed his arm as the bus passed them in a blur of motion.

Caleb listened for the sound of another vehicle.

"Do you see a black sedan?" he raised his voice so Samuel could hear his question.

"Some distance back. These are the men you are trying to elude?"

"If they attempt to stop the buggy, ignore their efforts. They are up to no good."

"Our turn is just ahead. Surely they will follow the bus."

That was Caleb's hope, as well. He held his breath as Samuel angled his buggy into the turn. Caleb glanced back. The car was approaching the turn.

Lizzie's face was drawn with worry. She bowed her head as if in prayer, which was what they needed at the moment.

"Come on, girl," Samuel encouraged his mare. "Get going."

Caleb counted his heartbeats to help control the tension that was bubbling up inside him and listened for the sound of wheels on pavement.

At long last, the dark sedan rushed past the turnoff.

Caleb let out the breath he was holding. Lizzie did the same.

They had completed the first hurdle, but Caleb wondered if the security guards would remember the Amish buggy and come back to search for Lizzie?

Samuel flicked his whip and the mare increased her pace. The faster they got to Samuel's farm, the faster they could hire the Amish taxi and ride to his aunt and uncle's house. Surely they would be safe there—or would security be able to find them even when they were hiding Amish?

TEN

By the time the buggy pulled into Samuel's farm, Lizzie's legs were almost numb from sitting on the floor for so long. She needed to work the kinks out of her stiff muscles before they started the next portion of their journey.

In spite of her own discomfort, she smiled, hearing the squeals of children who greeted the buggy as it came to a stop. Two towhead boys and an adorable little girl stood expectantly on the porch. Samuel climbed from the buggy and beckoned them forward. He wrapped each child in his arms as they giggled with glee and then scurried back to the porch.

The warmth of Samuel's embrace touched Lizzie's heart. How she had longed for her own father to greet her with such outward expressions of love.

"You must come inside and meet my wife," Samuel said to them. "The journey has been difficult. Now you can relax."

Caleb climbed down and helped Lizzie from the buggy. She was grateful to stand again and rubbed her neck.

"The floor of the buggy is not as comfortable as the bench, *yah*?" Samuel offered an apologetic smile.

"We are grateful for the ride," Caleb said.

An Amish women, small in stature with honey-brown hair and big blue eyes, stepped from the house, carrying a baby in her arms. "Welcome to you all."

Samuel quickly introduced Caleb and Lizzie to Ruth, his wife. "They are headed to Freemont. I told them Victor would drive them there."

"You must come inside. I have fresh baked cookies and the coffee is hot. This would be *gut*, *yah*?"

"*Yah.*" Lizzie stepped toward the porch. "Coffee and cookies sound *wunderbaar.*"

Caleb turned to Samuel. "I need to talk to the taxi driver, if you can show me where he lives."

"Come, we will go there together." Samuel pointed to a small house on the opposite side of the road. "The coffee and cookies can wait until we return."

"I saw Victor come home about an hour ago," Ruth called after them.

Lizzie followed her into the large kitchen.

Ruth spread a blanket on the floor and laid the baby in the middle of the soft flannel. The children came inside and sat next to the little one. Ruth motioned for Lizzie to sit at the table.

"You have been traveling long?" she asked.

"A number of hours."

"We are happy to have you here."

Lizzie glanced around the kitchen, noting the wood-burning cook stove with a counter on one side and a sideboard on the other. A funeral home calendar hung on the wall under a shelf holding an oil lamp. A square of tin reflected the light into the room, and a second lamp sat on an identical shelf on the far side of the sink, all of which reminded Lizzie of her home on Amish Mountain.

The apartment she shared with Sally had felt constrictive at times. Today, she enjoyed the open, utilitarian feel of the Amish home. The smell of baked cookies hung in the air along with the scent of coffee.

Ruth poured a cup for Lizzie and placed a plate of cookies on the table in front of her.

"We will have soup and sandwiches for *nacht-esse*." Ruth handed each of her older children a cookie. "There is more than enough if you care to join us for the evening meal."

"Thank you, Ruth, but we need to continue our journey."

Lizzie glanced at the children sitting quietly on the floor by the baby. "You have a lovely family."

"Children are a blessing. You and Caleb will have your own soon enough, I feel sure."

"Oh, we are—" Lizzie stopped herself. An unmarried man and woman traveling alone was not in keeping with the Amish way. She could understand Ruth's confusion.

"Caleb and I are friends and are both traveling home."

"You are to be wed soon?"

Lizzie's cheeks warmed. "We are friends."

"Yet I see something in your eyes when you talk about him."

Was her attraction to Caleb that obvious?

Steps sounded on the porch. The women turned as the door opened and Samuel and Caleb entered the kitchen.

"Victor will be ready to drive them within the hour. Fill two more cups, Ruth. We have enough time to enjoy the cookies with our coffee."

Lizzie liked Samuel and his wife. Their children were adorable and well-behaved, and she wished they could spend more time with the delightful family. Relaxing in their Amish house, even for a short time, brought comfort in the midst of her upset about searching for Emma.

"It was so good of you to invite us into your home," Lizzie said when the Amish taxi arrived at the door.

Caleb and Samuel shook hands and Ruth embraced her with a warm hug. "It is our hope that we would see you again," she said as they walked to the porch. The children gathered around their parents, seemingly too shy to speak.

Lizzie felt sad as she slipped into the rear of the taxi. Caleb sat next to her and they both waved goodbye through the open window.

"Safe travel," Samuel called to them as the taxi left the drive and turned onto the country road.

That was what Lizzie wanted. Safe travel and a way to find Emma.

She sighed deeply and closed her eyes.

She had to focus on finding Emma. That and nothing else.

Not the long journey or the security guards looking for her or how much she appreciated Caleb's help. Nothing mattered except finding Emma.

ELEVEN

Caleb could not relax. He kept his gaze on the road ahead of them, then turned frequently to ensure they were not being followed.

He had seen the black sedan speed along the highway, but he knew the guards would eventually realize following the bus had been a mistake.

They were focused on Lizzie and would stop at nothing to find her. The thought made his gut rumble.

He glanced at her on the seat next to him. Her eyes were closed, and she appeared to be drifting into a light slumber. He scooted closer and allowed his arm to touch hers. Without opening her eyes, she dropped her head to his shoulder and snuggled close.

Her long lashes fanned her cheeks, and her breathing was shallow and steady in spite of the twists and turns in the country road.

Caleb wasn't sure how much to tell his aunt and uncle about Lizzie. Less would be best at first, until he was certain of their willingness to help.

His eyes grew heavy, and he drifted to sleep, then jerked awake when the taxi braked at a four-way stop. Night had fallen, and Caleb was unsure of where they were.

He learned forward, using care not to wake

Lizzie, and tapped the driver's shoulder. "Are we close?"

"Another couple miles."

He settled back again. Lizzie's eyes fluttered open. She gazed up at him and smiled. His breath hitched, and a warmth spread throughout his body.

As if realizing she was resting her head on his shoulder, Lizzie bolted upright and frowned apologetically. He hated to have her pull away from him and felt an instant chill from their separation.

"Forgive me, Caleb. I did not mean to use your shoulder as a pillow."

"It was not a problem. You were tired. I slept, as well."

She glanced outside. "It is dark already?"

"We will be at our destination in a mile or so."

Lizzie rubbed her hand over her stomach. "Now I am nervous about meeting your aunt and uncle."

"There is no reason to be concerned. My aunt will love having another woman in the house, and my uncle will enjoy a second set of hands to help with the farm chores."

"Have they traveled to Willkommen to visit your family?"

"A few times when I was young, but my father was less than welcoming."

"That must be hard on your mother."

"She would like the family to gather together,

but it does not happen. Still, my aunt and uncle were most gracious when I visited them last year."

"I'm sure they enjoyed your company."

Caleb had lived alone for almost three years and had isolated himself from the Pinecraft Amish community. Like an outsider, he had watched the vacationers ride their tricycles and enjoy their leisure time. The men often played chess at the park. Shuffleboard was another popular pastime.

Instead of taking part in the community activities, he had holed up in his cottage most evenings. At night, he would sit on the front stoop and whittle. Amish couples frequently walked past his house with their children. Seeing their contentment made him long for a family of his own. Being with Lizzie made that longing even more pronounced.

When he left home, he had also left his faith, yet he had not totally accepted the *Englisch* life. Not knowing where he belonged caused confusion since he could not see himself in either setting. If not Amish and not *Englisch*, then where would he find his spot?

He wondered what Lizzie would choose for her own future. There was a wide chasm between the two ways of life. If Lizzie returned to the Amish faith, their paths would part again, which troubled Caleb.

"You look upset." Lizzie stared at him as she

raked her hair back from her face and stretched her shoulders. "Are you worried about seeing your relatives?"

"Not at all, but I was thinking of their Amish life. I am not sure I want to enter into it again."

"You are doing so because of me, Caleb, for which I am grateful."

"I am doing it so we can help a friend who is in danger."

"Of course, it is because of Emma. As soon as we find her, I will leave so as not to confuse your life."

Once again, Caleb did not understand her comment. "You do not confuse anything."

He was the one who was confused about the future.

Amish or *Englisch*? Caleb wasn't sure.

Lizzie regretted falling asleep on Caleb's shoulder. Waking to find him so close had thrown her inner calm into chaos. For a long moment, she had not known where she was and could only see Caleb looking bigger than life and so very handsome.

Even more unsettling, she had thought she was dreaming and had started to raise her lips to his. Thankfully, she came to her senses in time to realize she was *not* dreaming. The thought of what she could have done made her cheeks burn and her pulse pound with nervous embarrassment.

His cool demeanor confirmed that Caleb had not been affected in the slightest by her nearness. The only one who thought the situation unsettling was her. She felt like an *Englisch* schoolgirl dreaming of knights in shining armor. Lizzie was confident no one—not even Caleb Zook with his dark brown eyes and full lips—would steal her heart. Although if truth be told, he already had.

Yet he was almost betrothed to her best friend, which made Lizzie even more confused and brought her back to the problem at hand. How would she find Emma?

The taxi turned into a drive and parked in front of a large farmhouse situated back from the road. Moonlight filtered over the two rocking chairs on the front porch. Mums and a flurry of yellow pansies waved from the front walk in the night breeze. Caleb's aunt must like to garden.

Lizzie's mother enjoyed flowers, but her father said they took time away from the chores at hand. Her mother never went against her father's wishes. Neither had Lizzie, until she left home.

She thought of the police interrogation the morning after Emma had gone missing. Her father's hand had rested on Lizzie's shoulder as she told law enforcement what her *datt* had prompted her to say about accompanying Emma to the beach that night. Her father had forbid her from admitting the fact that she had started the chain of events that led to Emma's disappearance. The memory of her own complicity made Lizzie's heart beat so fast she thought Caleb would surely hear it pounding almost out of her chest.

He squeezed her hand as if he realized her upset. She had never known anyone who sensed her need even before she realized it herself. Now here she was on a remote Amish farm with a man she hadn't seen for over three years.

What would her father say if he knew? As Caleb had mentioned, sometimes it was better that her parents did not know what she was doing.

Swallowing down the nervous bile that filled her throat, she straightened her spine as Caleb stepped from the car and hurried to open her door. With his hand on her arm, he said goodbye to the taxi driver and then guided her toward the porch.

"What about paying him?" she asked.

"I paid him earlier."

"I owe you," she whispered as the kitchen door opened.

"Who is there?" A beefy man, early fifties, stepped onto the porch. He held a lantern in his hand and blinked in the night.

"It is Caleb, Uncle Zach."

"Caleb! Such a wonderful surprise! Martha, look who comes to visit us again."

With a wide grin on his face, Caleb stepped forward as his aunt hurried outside, her arms wide. She ran down the steps to embrace him.

Her warm welcome touched Lizzie's heart. She stood quietly to the side, not wanting to interrupt the lovely homecoming that was playing out before her.

As his aunt patted Caleb's shoulder and pulled him even closer, she spied Lizzie. The woman's eyes widened.

"Who is this you have brought with you, Caleb?"

He turned and motioned Lizzie forward. "Lizzie Kauffman, Aunt Martha. She is from Willkommen. We knew each other in our youth."

"You have been home to visit your *datt*?" she asked.

He shook his head. "I have remained in Pinecraft. Lizzie came there and we met by accident."

His aunt looked puzzled, as if trying to piece the parts together to determine who Lizzie was. No doubt unable to come to a logical conclusion, she shrugged, smiled widely and opened her arms to Lizzie.

The woman's massive hug took her aback. For a long moment, Lizzie stood still, then the love that emanated from the older Amish woman surrounded Lizzie like a thick blanket on a cold winter's night. She giggled, not with embarrassment but with a sense of joy and well-being and thankfulness for the genuine welcome that touched her to the core.

"We are glad you can be with us, Lizzie. You

are tired from your trip and hungry, *yah*? I fixed a stew and more than we needed."

She glanced at her husband. "Zachariah asked why I cooked so much and I did not have an answer, although now I know what *Gott* was telling me. He was whispering in my ear that family was coming to visit."

Family. Lizzie loved the sound of the word as it rolled off Martha's tongue.

Uncle Zach motioned Lizzie and Caleb toward the house. "Come inside. Mother has hot coffee and a *gut nachtesse.*"

"Thank you," she said, as she followed them into the open kitchen. Delicious smells of garlic, onions and tomatoes filled the house, as well as something baking in the oven.

"*Ack.* I almost forgot the dinner rolls." Aunt Martha wrapped a dish towel protectively around her hand before she opened the oven.

The aroma of fresh baked rolls made Lizzie's mouth water. She hadn't realized how hungry she was.

"I will set two more places at the table," Martha said.

"Are you sure it's not a problem?" Lizzie asked.

"I told you there is plenty, and a full table brings me joy."

"At least let me help."

Aunt Martha nodded. "The silverware is in

the drawer by the sink. The napkins are in the basket."

Lizzie found the utensils and also placed two additional glasses and coffee mugs on the table.

"Pour the coffee, dear. The pot is hot." Aunt Martha hesitated for a moment. "It is not too soon to eat?"

"Never," Caleb said, patting his aunt's shoulder. "We have traveled all day and are eager to enjoy your cooking."

"Caleb, you always were a sweet boy. You take after your mother."

The aunt dished up plates, and Lizzie placed them on the table.

"It is nice to have help," his aunt said with a grateful smile.

Martha motioned them to the table. Uncle Zach took his seat and lowered his head. Lizzie followed his lead and gave thanks for their trip to this home and for the warm welcome she felt, as well as the hearty stew they were about to eat. Her stomach gurgled in anticipation.

"It sounds as if you are hungry." Uncle Zach laughed as he placed a napkin on his lap.

"Evidently what you say is true. Everything looks delicious, Mr.—"

"Call me Uncle Zach, and my wife is Aunt Martha."

Martha smiled in agreement as she passed the

rolls. Lizzie took one and handed the basket to Caleb.

"Your trip was uneventful?" his aunt asked.

Caleb nodded. "The bus took us to a rest stop just off the highway. We caught a ride with an Amish man to his house and he told us about the Amish taxi."

"I am surprised the bus did not stop at Freemont, which would have been so much closer."

"Perhaps another bus would do so."

Lizzie ate the stew in silence, wondering when they would reveal their reason for being here. Would Caleb's aunt and uncle be as gracious if they knew the truth about their visit? Tomorrow she would encourage Caleb to explain their need to find Emma. Until then, Lizzie would accept their outreach and be grateful for their hospitality.

She was glad to have a place to stay away from Pinecraft and the Estate Security guards. Surely they would not trace her to this Amish farm in rural South Georgia. At least that was her hope.

TWELVE

Caleb rose early the next morning and hurried downstairs, hoping to talk to his uncle before he left the house.

His aunt smiled as he entered the kitchen. "You are ready for breakfast?"

"Yes, thank you, Aunt Martha. Is Uncle Zach around?"

"He's hitching the mare to the buggy."

"Is he going to town?"

"*Yah*, is there something you need?"

"I wanted to help with the chores."

"Hurry, you must catch him before he leaves."

Uncle Zach smiled as Caleb entered the barn. "I had hoped to rise early enough to help with the morning chores. Aunt Martha said you are going to town. What needs to be done?"

"The horses have already been fed and the dairy cows milked. Martha does it when I am gone, but she wanted to bake this morning so we would have a good lunch and dinner."

"What about the fences?"

"The south pasture needs some work. Also the chicken coop could stand to be shored up a bit more. We've seen a fox sneaking around, and I don't want to lose our laying hens or any of the meat hens. Fried chicken is one of my favorite meals."

"With Aunt Martha cooking, every meal is *gut, yah*?"

His uncle chuckled in agreement.

"Go to town," Caleb continued, "and do not worry about the farm. We will talk when you return home."

His uncle raised a brow. "There is something you wish to tell me?"

"Lizzie and I need to find an old friend who may be in trouble. We believe unscrupulous people are holding her against her will."

"This is a serious accusation, Caleb."

"Which I would not say unless it was true. For your safety and for ours, it would be better that you do not mention that Lizzie and I are visiting."

"This worries me."

"After your trip to town, we will share what we know with you and Aunt Martha." Caleb could tell his uncle was unsettled by the information.

"Stay alert," his uncle warned. "So that nothing happens while I am gone."

"Of course. You do not have to worry."

But as his uncle climbed into the buggy, Caleb knew there was much for which to worry.

"You slept well?" Aunt Martha asked when Lizzie hurried downstairs and stepped into the kitchen.

"Better than I have for days. Thank you. Something smells delicious."

"It is the breakfast biscuits. Would you put the butter and jam on the table?"

Lizzie did as the woman asked. "What about the henhouse? Shall I gather the eggs?"

"I collected them earlier."

Lizzie glanced through the window. "It is good to be back on a farm. You and Uncle Zach have such a nice place here."

"The only thing missing are children." Martha shook her head with regret. "I have been with child five times, but the babies did not survive."

"I am so sorry."

"*Gott* has gifted us with many blessings. This is a cross we are to carry."

Lizzie thought of her own life. What cross was she supposed to carry?

Caleb stepped into the kitchen, bringing with him the fresh scent of the outdoors. His eyes brightened and a smile tugged at his full mouth. Her heart fluttered, leaving her momentarily lightheaded so that she reached for the back of the chair.

"Are you all right?" he asked, concern evident in his tone.

"I am fine."

"You are hungry." His aunt looked at them both. "Breakfast is ready. Wash your hands, Caleb, and we will eat."

Martha pulled the biscuits from the oven and placed one on each of the plates and covered them with a hearty serving of ground beef and gravy. On Caleb's plate, she added two additional biscuits and piled them high with the meat mixture.

"You are sure to fatten me like the hogs you keep out back, Aunt Martha."

She laughed, noticeably pleased by his comment. "You are still young and need your energy. Uncle Zach cannot eat as much or it will go to his belly."

"It will go to mine, as well.

"*Pshaw*, you are talking like the *Englisch* who do not eat because they fear gaining weight. If they worked with their hands and did the chores Amish men tackle each day, they would not worry about calories."

Lizzie smiled as she grabbed the coffee pot and filled three mugs sitting on the counter. "You are right. And for the women too."

"Uncle Zach has missed another *gut* meal," Caleb said as he carried the mugs to the table.

"He ate early to get a start on the day. He took some of my jams and baked goods to sell at the Amish Market. The men gather there to share news and talk about the weather. He comes home in *gut* spirits."

"And you, Aunt Martha, do you not go to town?" Caleb asked.

"Some days I do, but I have my quilting group and *kaffeeklatsches* when the women gather. Plus, we see each other at Sunday church and when we visit. I do not need the comradery that your uncle does."

She motioned them to the table. Once seated, they bowed their heads. After a brief moment of private prayer, Lizzie raised her fork and sighed as she savored the rich flavors of the meat and gravy. "You are spoiling us, Aunt Martha."

"Spoiled with love is never a bad thing," she responded with a warm smile.

After breakfast, Lizzie washed the dishes and tidied the kitchen while Caleb finished the chores and then headed to the pasture to mend the fencing.

Aunt Martha mixed pie dough while Lizzie peeled and sliced the apples. Together they made four pies.

"Next we will bake bread. You will knead the dough?"

"Of course." Lizzie kneaded the dough and punched it down, then returned it to a greased bowl. She covered the bowl with a cloth and placed it on the back of the stove to keep warm.

Martha nodded her approval. "You know how to work the dough."

"I was the only daughter in a family of four boys. Much bread needed to be baked."

"No doubt you were your father's princess."

Lizzie was unsure how to respond. "I was the first born and always felt like a disappointment to my father. He was happy once his sons were born."

"And you are sensitive to his comments?"

Lizzie shrugged. "Perhaps."

Martha patted Lizzie's hand. "Your father should rejoice to have such a fine daughter."

While the dough rested on the back of the stove and the pies were baking, Martha cut up vegetables for soup and started a large pot to cook.

"You never stop working," Lizzie said.

"It is the way, *yah*? You, as well. I am grateful for your help. This afternoon, we could piece together quilt squares. I just started a new one to sell at the market."

"You and Uncle Zach work together."

Martha nodded. "It is the Amish way."

Lizzie tilted her head.

"Is it not like this in your family?" Martha asked.

"I should not speak ill of my parents."

"It is not speaking ill to speak the truth."

"I find too many Amish marriages are not based on love and respect."

"And this troubles you."

Lizzie nodded. "What I see makes me glad I am not married."

"Which makes me wonder if you are afraid to take a husband because of what you experienced in your home growing up? Is this the case?"

Afraid of marriage?

Caleb had mentioned Eli Beiler. A nice person, but she had no desire to spend the rest of her life at his side.

"You're jumping to the wrong conclusion, Aunt Martha."

"I see what I see."

"Meaning what?"

"Meaning I see how you look at Caleb."

"We are friends."

"Friends but something more lies buried beneath the surface, something you are not willing to admit because of how you view marriage."

"Why do you think that?"

Martha laughed. "I know people and can sense how others feel even without being told. You and Caleb are young. It is hard to know what the future will bring. Sometimes we do not see that which is good even when it is right before our eyes."

"Caleb is a *gut* man," Lizzie agreed. "But he has given his heart to another woman."

"Where is this woman, and why instead is he with you?"

Lizzie had said too much.

Caleb pushed open the door and stepped inside. His face was ruddy from the wind and winter sun.

"The fence is fixed."

"You work fast, Caleb. Thank you. Your uncle will be pleased."

"I saw him approaching on the road."

Aunt Martha raised her brow. "He is early to come home. I hope nothing is wrong."

The sound of the buggy turning onto the drive drew her to the window.

The clip-clop of the horse's hooves stopped, followed by footsteps on the porch. Zach's face was twisted with concern when he entered the kitchen. He looked first at Caleb and then at Lizzie. Her stomach flip-flopped as she noted his expression.

Something was wrong. Very, very wrong.

"You are home early." Aunt Martha helped him out of his coat.

"I wanted to ensure you were all right."

She laughed nervously. "Why would I not be all right?"

"Because of what I found out in town."

Lizzie's gut tightened. Caleb looked at her, his face drawn.

Caleb's uncle held a newspaper in his hand. "I did not expect to see this on the front page of the paper."

"What is it, dear?" Aunt Martha asked.

He dropped the paper onto the table. At the bottom of the front page was a photo. Lizzie stepped closer.

Aunt Martha gasped. "Oh, my."

"So tell me, Caleb, what do you know about this?" Zach pointed to the photograph.

Lizzie swallowed hard, seeing her own likeness as she ran from Mr. Thompson's estate.

"I can explain," Lizzie said.

"Tell me, first of all," Uncle Zach demanded. "Have you brought danger to our house?"

Lizzie's eyes burned with tears. The look on Uncle Zach's face told her she was not welcome and should leave immediately.

"I am sorry to cause you upset." She ran upstairs to pack her bag, but the tears began to fall and she tumbled onto the bed and cried for everything that had happened. Especially for Emma who had gotten mixed up with Andrew Thompson, a vile man who abused women, all because Lizzie wanted someone to notice her on the beach.

So much pain had transpired since that afternoon when she had openly flirted with the handsome playboy, never realizing what type of person he was and never thinking Emma would want to meet him later that night. Why hadn't Lizzie said no to the nighttime rendezvous? If only she had been strong enough to go against Emma's wishes.

Emma always got her way, but it wasn't Emma's fault. It was Lizzie's fault. She had been the one to teasingly agree to meet Andrew.

Lizzie had ruined her relationship with Caleb's aunt and uncle and had embarrassed him in spite of his desire to help.

She would pack her bag and leave, but where would she go? The only thing she was certain about was she had to find Emma.

THIRTEEN

Caleb tried to explain what had happened, but his aunt and uncle looked as if the story was too convoluted to believe.

"Lizzie appeared at your door in Pinecraft?" Aunt Martha repeated what he had told her.

He explained about Lizzie's need to learn what had happened to Emma and about her temporary employment that had landed her a job in the Thompson home.

"It seems too improbable," his uncle groused. "The girl is making this up."

"Uncle Zach, I believe her," Caleb insisted.

"You have known her long?" his uncle asked.

"All my life."

Aunt Martha touched Zach's arm. "She seems like a nice girl. Perhaps a bit confused and emotional now as she worries about her friend. I do not understand why she is wanted by the authorities."

Caleb did not understand why either. "It has to do with Thad Thompson." He explained about the wealthy man with the delinquent son and what he had possibly done to various women on the family's island.

"This is not something I wish to hear," his uncle said with a huff.

"It is reality, Uncle Zach. There are bad people in the world."

"*Yah*, with the Amish, as well. Still, I do not like that you are involved."

"I'm helping Lizzie. She has no one else." He explained what she had learned about Emma being held in a nursing home in the local area. "Have you heard of Respite Haven?"

His aunt's eyes widened. She raised her brow and glanced at her husband. "It is not far. Many of the Amish visit the elderly and infirmed who live there."

"Have you been there?" Caleb asked.

"*Yah*," she nodded. "I usually go once a month."

"That's where Emma is supposed to be. We need to ensure she is all right."

Uncle Zach shook his head. "Three years is a long time."

"And if it weren't for Lizzie, we would not have found out where Emma has been all this time."

Caleb's aunt poured a cup of coffee and handed it to her husband. "You have jumped to the wrong conclusion, Zachariah."

"I thought you were in danger," he offered as an excuse.

"Lizzie would not hurt anyone," Caleb insisted.

"See to her," Martha said, pointing to the stairs. "Tell her I am making lunch if she will find it in her heart to forgive us."

Caleb hurried upstairs and knocked on the guest-room door. "Lizzie?"

He heard a shuffle of footsteps before the door pulled open. She stood in front of him, eyes red and face puffy. His heart broke seeing her upset.

She blinked back more tears. "I will pack my bag and leave as soon as possible, Caleb. Will you drive me to town in your uncle's buggy?"

He held up his hand. "My uncle wishes to apologize for his hasty remarks. I explained what has happened and that the news article is incorrect."

"But does he believe you?"

"He does, and he is sorry that his words caused you pain. He was fearful for my aunt's safety and acted out of his concern instead of waiting to learn the truth from you. Aunt Martha is fixing lunch. She wants you to come downstairs."

"But—"

"No buts. It is as I said. You must forgive their impetuousness."

"I do not want to bring problems to their home."

"Then you will come downstairs?"

"After I compose myself. Tell your aunt I will be downstairs soon."

She closed the door. Caleb stood in the hallway, chastising himself for not explaining everything to his uncle last night. Instead, he had waited until he and Lizzie could talk to them together. Regrettably, he had waited too long.

His heart ached for Lizzie. She had suffered for the last three years just as he had, only Caleb knew that by rejecting Emma, he had caused her to go to the yacht with Andrew Thompson, which meant everything that had happened to Lizzie was his fault, as well.

He did not want to join his aunt and uncle at the moment. Instead, he went into the guest room where he had slept last night and sat on the bed. Dropping his head in his hands, he inwardly moaned.

How could good come from all that had happened. Even if they found Emma, she would be a different person. Injured perhaps from the beating but also warped by her isolation.

Caleb had ruined Emma's life, as well as Lizzie's and his own. He was to blame for everything that had happened.

Lizzie poured water into the ceramic washbowl on the dresser in her room and splashed the cool liquid over her hot face. She knew her eyes were bloodshot, and her cheeks splotched from crying. Her father scolded her when she cried, so she had learned to hold back her own hurt in obedience to him. He would chastise her if he saw her tears today.

Perhaps Caleb's uncle felt the same.

A tap sounded at her door.

Expecting to see Caleb, she pulled it open. His

aunt stood with a cup in her hand. "Tea makes me feel better when I am upset," she said, offering the mug.

"I'm sorry, Aunt Martha."

"We are the ones who must beg your forgiveness. Zachariah jumped to the wrong conclusion. He believed what he read in the newspaper instead of finding out the truth from you and Caleb. He asks forgiveness."

"There is no reason for Uncle Zach to ask forgiveness. He opened his home to me without knowing who I was and the history of why Caleb and I were here. We should have been forthright."

"We will start fresh, *yah*?"

Her smile was as warm as the mug in Lizzie's hand. Without hesitation, she stepped into the woman's outstretched arms.

"We are glad you are with us, Lizzie. We wish you to remain for as long as you can. This is from my heart, and my husband agrees."

"You are too generous, Aunt Martha. I need to find Emma and then I will leave."

"Caleb mentioned Respite Haven. I have a plan as to how you will locate your friend."

"You do?"

Caleb's aunt nodded. "Come downstairs. We will discuss what needs to be done after lunch."

"You are sure?"

"Of this, I am certain." Martha squeezed her hand before she returned to the kitchen.

Lizzie found Caleb waiting for her in the hallway. He stretched out his hand. "We will go downstairs together."

Uncle Zach was standing at the table and hurried to greet them. "I ask your forgiveness, Lizzie. I believed what I read in the paper without thinking of what it could really mean."

"I am sorry that I reacted so strongly, Uncle Zach. Of course, you would be worried, thinking I had done something wrong."

"Caleb told us what has happened. This is a terrible situation, and we know you are worried about your friend."

"She is at Respite Haven," Martha added. "We will go there tomorrow."

"What?" Lizzie could not believe what she'd heard.

"A group of Amish visit each month. We have gone before. The men play checkers or chess with the residents while the ladies socialize. It cheers their day."

"Did you see a young Amish woman with blond hair and blue eyes?" Lizzie asked.

"We have seen young people there, but no one fitting that description, although we only started visiting six months ago. Other people have been going for years. We can ask them if they know of this friend of yours."

"We must be careful," Uncle Zach cautioned. "I will drive the buggy. Lizzie, you will sit in the rear. Once we arrive, there will be many Amish gathered outside before we enter the home. You will blend in. With a bonnet, it is doubtful you will be recognized."

That was Lizzie's hope. In spite of Uncle Zach's earlier upset, she was elated. Three years was a long time, but everything would end on a positive note when—and if—she found Emma.

FOURTEEN

Caleb couldn't sleep that night. Needing fresh air, he took the lantern and went outside. He found a block of wood and began to whittle by the light of the lantern. The cool air cleared his mind and working with his hands untangled some of his confusion.

If only all of life's problems could be solved by whittling. Eventually, he returned inside and climbed the stairs. He glanced at Lizzie's room, but at this late hour, he would not bother her. He wanted her to sleep and wake refreshed. Tomorrow would be a long day filled with either joy or pain. He hoped the former. Lizzie would need to be rested and alert. He would have to be alert, as well.

The next morning, Caleb was up before dawn and outside tending to the livestock before his uncle crawled from bed. The older man met him in the barn.

"You have gotten a head start on the day, Caleb."

"We are going to the nursing home. I did not want the chores to languish."

"I appreciate your help. I had trouble sleeping last night after the upset I caused Lizzie. I must not be so hasty in my judgments."

"I too had trouble sleeping because of her,

but it was worry about what we might find and whether someone might identify her from the photograph in the newspaper."

"She was not dressed Amish in the paper. It is doubtful people will make the connection. The photo was taken at night and somewhat blurred."

"Yet you recognized her, Uncle."

"*Yah*, you are right. Still, we will not let her go off on her own today. There is security in numbers."

Caleb hoped what his uncle said would prove true.

Lizzie's stomach was in turmoil as she raced downstairs. Aunt Martha had biscuits baking and was frying slices of ham in a cast-iron skillet.

"What can I do to help?" Lizzie asked.

"Set the table and bring me the basket of eggs. It is by the door."

"I slept too late. If I had awakened earlier, I could have gathered the eggs for you."

"The men were out before first light. I could not remain in bed, knowing they would need breakfast. The hens left their eggs in easy-to-find nests so it did not take me long."

She glanced at the door. "The butter and milk are in the cold water by the pump. Wrap a cape around your shoulders and fetch them if you need something to do."

"Gladly." Lizzie did as Aunt Martha requested.

The cool morning air greeted her, and she hurried to the bucket. After lifting out the jars of butter and milk, she wiped them on a towel and returned to the house.

"The jam is on the counter," Martha said. "Take that to the table along with the butter. Then pour the milk into a pitcher."

"You are cooking so much this morning."

"We will pack sandwiches and not eat again until after our visit to Respite Haven. I wanted to fix something warm and hearty that would stick to our ribs this morning."

Aunt Martha transferred the bacon to a plate and placed it on the rear of the stovetop to keep warm. "See if the men can stop long enough to eat," she requested.

"I will tell them breakfast is almost ready."

Lizzie hurried to the barn and called out to Caleb. "Can you make time for breakfast? Aunt Martha is ready to fry the eggs."

"I'll get my uncle. Tell her we will be there as soon as we wash up." He hesitated for a moment and then added, "Did you sleep well?"

"On and off. I heard you go downstairs and worried you might be upset. Then I saw you whittling by the light of the lantern. It was a cold night to be outside."

"Yet the work cleared my head and allowed me to finally sleep when I returned to my room."

"You are worried about today?" she asked.

"I am concerned about what we might find."

"You mean in addition to Emma?"

"I mean Estate Security and perhaps Mr. Thompson himself or his son, Andrew. You must assure me you will be on guard the entire time and not do anything foolish."

"What I did that was foolish was agreeing to go to the beach with Emma three years ago. Nothing compares with that, which is why I need to reconcile myself with my failing."

"It was not your fault."

"So you say, but you do not know all that had happened that day."

He stared at her for a long moment as if waiting for her to reveal something more, but she was not ready to go into what had happened, not when Aunt Martha was waiting to cook the eggs and serve a hot meal to the men.

"Tell Uncle Zach it is time to eat." She hurried back to the kitchen.

Aunt Martha glanced up as Lizzie entered. "The men are not yet ready?"

"They must wash before joining us in the kitchen."

Lizzie hung the cape on the wall peg, washed her hands and poured coffee in the cups on the table.

Returning the pot to the stove, she glanced outside, seeing both men at the pump.

Caleb was tall and muscular and laughed at

something his uncle said. They seemed to have a *gut* relationship and she wondered, for half a second, what was so funny. She had not laughed in so long and she wanted to forget the seriousness of what they were about to do and instead lose herself in a frivolous moment.

Martha cracked eggs into the hot grease that sizzled and popped. "You will find a few tins of cookies in the pantry. We will take them with us. The residents enjoy the baked items along with their coffee."

Lizzie found the tins and placed them on the counter.

Uncle Zach hurried inside, bringing with him a rush of cold morning air. Caleb followed, his cheeks ruddy from the morning air. His sleeves were rolled up and his arms were still damp.

Lizzie handed him a towel.

"*Danki.*" His smile warmed her heart.

Much as she worried about what they would find today, it was time to face the past, as well as Emma. Whatever came of it would be better than not knowing where Emma was.

If only she were of sound mind and not infirmed. They would know the truth about her soon, and all of Lizzie's struggles would come to an end. At least she hoped the new day would dawn with the promise of a future filled with joy.

FIFTEEN

After breakfast, Caleb helped his uncle finish the chores. At ten o'clock, they hitched Daisy to the buggy and guided the mare to the back of the house.

The kitchen door opened and Aunt Martha hurried outside, carrying a number of tins and a basket of sandwiches.

"Let me help," Caleb said, taking the items from her hands.

His uncle assisted his wife into the buggy. Caleb arranged the tins and basket in the rear, then turned as Lizzie stepped onto the porch.

"Lock the door, dear," his aunt called.

Lizzie did as requested and tugged on the door to ensure it held.

"Locking the door is not something we usually do," Martha said. "Under the circumstances, it is wise to be cautious."

Lizzie left the porch and headed to the buggy. "Again, I am sorry to put you in this position."

"We are not concerned for our own safety but for yours," his uncle said.

Caleb put his hands on Lizzie's arm and helped her into the buggy. "We will sit on the second seat," he told her.

She settled into the seat and accepted the blanket his aunt offered. "Wrap this around your legs, dear. It is cold today."

Caleb crawled in beside Lizzie and smiled as she arranged the blanket over his legs, as well.

"The cold does not bother me," he assured her.

"Perhaps not, but I will worry less about you if your legs are covered."

He appreciated her concern and thoughtfulness and enjoyed sitting next to her. She smelled clean and fresh with a hint of lavender that made him want to scoot even closer. He took her hand and rubbed it between his own. "You should be wearing gloves."

"When we left Florida, I did not think the temperature would drop this low."

"North Georgia would be even colder, especially on Amish Mountain."

"It is one reason I am glad we moved to the Freemont area," his aunt said from the front, no doubt overhearing their comments.

"But we have more heat here in the summer months," Uncle Zach added.

"Still," Aunt Martha said with a nod. "A warmer winter suits me better."

As Caleb continued to rub Lizzie's hand, he wondered where she would go once Emma was found. Home to North Georgia or would she remain in the Freemont area, close to Caleb's aunt and uncle?

And what would he do? Return to Pinecraft? He

thought of whittling on the front porch and watching the families pass by on their evening walks. For some reason, that thought made him sad.

"We are drawing close," Uncle Zach said from the front of the buggy.

Lizzie gripped Caleb's hand and turned to stare into his eyes. "We will find her. We have to."

His face was drawn. Lizzie wished she could read his thoughts.

In the distance, she saw a sprawling one-story building with two wings that spanned out from the center.

A number of buggies were tethered to the hitching rails, and Amish men and women milled around the grassy area in front of the nursing home. Some of the couples waved as Zach pulled his buggy to a stop. He hitched the mare and helped Aunt Martha down. She hugged the women before taking the tins from Caleb. He jumped down and assisted Lizzie.

His aunt introduced them to the other couples and said Lizzie was a friend of their family, without providing her last name. The woman in the newspaper article was dressed *Englisch* and named Elizabeth Kauffman. Nowhere in the story was the name Lizzie mentioned.

The Amish people were enjoying their time together, and although welcoming, they did not pay undue attention to a newcomer named Lizzie, for which she was grateful.

For a long moment, she stared at the care facility, all the while holding her hand against her stomach in hopes of stilling the butterflies that fluttered inside her. Turning slowly, she glanced at the cars in the parking lot, searching for a black sedan with tinted windows and was relieved to find no such vehicle in the lot.

The door to Respite Haven opened and a pretty nurse waved from the doorway. "Come in from the cold. Everyone is eager for your visit."

"Our first task is to help the residents to the dining room," Aunt Martha explained to Lizzie as they stepped into the central foyer. "While they eat lunch, we will prepare the main hall for a social time following the meal."

A large pine tree in the lobby was decorated in twinkling lights and gold and red bulbs. A wreath tied with a pretty bow hung over the mantel of the stone fireplace, and Christmas carols played softly in the background. Respite Haven was clean and the furnishings appeared comfortable and fairly new.

Lizzie peered into a number of rooms. Most of the residents were elderly and infirmed, some bedridden, others sat in wheelchairs. A few folks used walkers to steady themselves.

Aunt Martha pointed to one of the rooms where two men waited in their wheelchairs. "We'll start on this end of the west wing and work our way to the dining area. Ask the residents if they need help getting to lunch."

Lizzie and Caleb pushed the men to the dining room and then split up as they assisted other folks.

At the end of the hallway, Lizzie caught a glimpse of a slender woman with blond hair. Hoping she had found Emma, Lizzie hurried into the room but instantly realized her mistake. The woman was at least thirty years older than Emma.

"Lunch will be served soon." Lizzie tried to mask her disappointment. "Do you need help getting to the dining room?"

"No thank you, hon. I'm able to walk there by myself."

"Your pretty hair reminds me of a friend of mine. She's twenty years old with blue eyes and blond hair. Do you know of any residents who match that description?"

"Pamela McQueen is blond and blue-eyed. Plus, she's about that age. Her room is at the end of the east wing."

Lizzie returned to the hallway, eager to tell Caleb the news. She spied him escorting a frail gentleman, who gripped his arm for support. Knowing he would be occupied for some time, she decided to find Emma on her own. Almost giddy with excitement, she rushed back to the central foyer and then headed into the east wing.

A tall slender man with graying hair and black glasses stood outside one of the rooms. He wore a white long-sleeve shirt, navy tie and a red vest. She tried to read his name tag as she past him, but the lanyard around his neck was flipped over.

"May I help you?" he asked.

She stopped abruptly and smiled, all the while trying to think of a satisfying reason she was in the east wing without mentioning Emma.

"I am here with the Amish volunteers," she finally said. "We are taking the residents to the dining room. Someone mentioned a person on this hallway who needed help."

He eyed her over the top of his glasses. "And who would that be?"

"Pamela McQueen."

"Pamela doesn't eat in the dining room." He pointed in the direction Lizzie had just come. "You need to return to the west wing. The patients on this wing do not take part in the visitor gatherings."

"Would you mind if I say hello to Pamela?"

He pursed his thin lips. "I'm afraid that wouldn't be a good idea. You could write her a card and send it here to Respite Haven. Pamela enjoys getting mail."

Lizzie looked fleetingly toward the last room on the left. The man cleared his throat as if to regain her attention. Seeing the determination on his face, she had no choice but to comply with his request.

Again, she glanced at the back of his name tag.

He extended his hand. "My name is Warren Whitaker. I'm the manager."

She gulped. Andrew Thompson's uncle.

Lizzie hoped he didn't notice her trembling as she accepted his handshake.

"Thank you for visiting the residents." He smiled halfheartedly. "They always enjoy the social time with the Amish community."

Frustrated that she had been stopped before finding Emma, Lizzie retraced her steps and found Caleb outside the dining room.

"I know where Emma is," she announced.

"Where?"

"In the east wing. She's going by the name Pamela McQueen."

Now she needed to find a way to get to Emma's room without being seen.

SIXTEEN

After the noon meal, the volunteers helped the residents into the main hall. The men set up board games and a quartet of Amish women sang Christmas carols. Caleb played checkers with a few of the men, while Lizzie poured punch and served cookies.

The time passed quickly and as the social was drawing to a close, Caleb approached Lizzie. "Let's try to find Emma."

She started for the door when Caleb grabbed her hand.

"Change of plans. We'll stay here for now."

"What?" She looked confused.

He pointed to the window. A dark sedan had pulled to the curb and two men stepped from the vehicle. Both of them wore khaki slacks and blue polos.

"Estate Security," Lizzie whispered. "How did they find us?"

"They're probably here to check on Emma or talk to Mr. Thompson's brother-in-law."

"Suppose they see us?"

"My guess is they won't recognize either of us dressed in Amish clothing."

Caleb didn't see any way to elude the guards. Their best option was to remain where they were and blend in with the crowd.

As he watched, the men approached the main hall entryway. An aide unlatched the door and invited them inside.

Lizzie kept staring at the men and accidently overfilled a cup with the punch she was pouring. Aunt Martha grabbed a nearby cloth and wiped up the spill.

The guards said something to the aide who motioned for them to follow her. She headed to the refreshment table where Lizzie stood. Raising her brow, she offered each man a glass of punch.

One of the men shook his head, but the second guard, stocky with a military buzz cut, reached for a drink just as Lizzie set another filled cup on the table. Their hands collided, splashing more punch onto the already soiled tablecloth.

Caleb grimaced.

Lizzie smiled weakly and handed the guard a fresh cup. "Help yourself to the baked items," she enthused. "They're all homemade."

The man nodded his thanks, took two cookies and then followed his partner and the aide into the main hallway.

Caleb exhaled the breath he was holding. Lizzie seemed to deflate, as well.

She hurried to where Caleb stood. "The aide mentioned a meeting with Mr. Whitaker. They'll be tied up in his office. This is our opportunity to find Emma."

When the aide returned to the meeting room,

Caleb handed her a glass of punch. "We would like to take punch and cookies to the residents in the east wing."

"That would be nice."

"What about the manager?"

"He's in a closed door meeting, but I'll be happy to escort you into the other wing."

Caleb nodded to Lizzie. They grabbed a tray, loaded it with cookies and cups of punch and followed the aide past the main office area. A sign on one of the doors read Warren Whitaker, Respite Haven Manager.

"We saw a couple gentlemen enter the hall earlier," Caleb mentioned. "They didn't look like local folks."

"I'm not sure who they are. Mr. Thompson owns the facility and plans to visit Respite Haven in the next couple of days. The men might be coordinating his arrival."

"Mr. Thompson must be an amazing man," Lizzie said.

The aide nodded. "He's certainly built a lot of nursing homes in rural areas that were without facilities for the infirmed and aged. The people in Freemont are grateful for Respite Haven. It means the world to a lot of families who needed care for their loved ones."

"Do you know exactly when Mr. Thompson will visit Respite Haven?" Lizzie pressed.

"I'm not sure. Over the past few months, we've

done a number of renovations to get the place looking good. A little paint can make a big difference."

Lizzie and Caleb distributed snacks to some of the residents, but before they reached the room at the end of the hallway, the aide glanced at her watch. "I didn't realize the time. The social will be over soon. We should head back to the main hall."

"We have a few more cookies and some punch left. What about the resident in the last room?" Lizzie asked.

"I'm not sure if Pamela is there. Most afternoons she has physical therapy."

"She's had an injury?"

"It was a car accident. Therapy helps, but only so much can be done for traumatic brain injury."

"We'll leave the punch and cookies in her room if she's not there," Caleb suggested.

"That would be fine." The aide glanced again at her watch. "I need to get back to the hall. You'll be all right without me?"

"Of course. Thanks for your help."

As the aide hurried away, Caleb and Lizzie tapped on Pamela's door, then opened it ever so slightly.

"Ms. McQueen?"

A door slammed behind them. Caleb glanced at the central lobby. Mr. Whitaker stood talking to the security guards.

Fearing they would be seen, Caleb thrust Lizzie into Pamela's room. His gut tightened. Or was it Emma's room?

Lizzie' heart nearly pounded out of her chest. A woman sat in a chair near her bed with her back to the door. Three years had passed, but Lizzie recognized Emma's slender form and the color of her hair.

Caleb's eyes widened as if he weren't ready to reconnect with Emma.

Leaving him to work out his own struggle, Lizzie stepped forward, touched the woman's arm and leaned closer to her chair. "Emma. It's Lizzie. I've been searching for you."

The woman turned. Confusion lined her face. She glanced at Lizzie and then smiled at Caleb.

He moaned.

"Do I know either of you?" the woman asked.

Her eyes were dark blue with specks of green. Her nose was aquiline and her lips thin.

The woman was not Emma.

"We brought you some punch and cookies," Lizzie said, blinking back tears of disappointment.

The door opened and Mr. Whitaker stepped into the room. "You again! Did I not tell you patients on this wing do not take part in the activities?"

Her heart raced. "Yes, sir. I'm sorry. One of the aides said Pamela might like a treat."

She stepped past Mr. Whitaker with Caleb following close behind her.

"Your group is leaving," the manager called out to them. "You need to leave, as well."

Lizzie and Caleb met Aunt Martha and Uncle Zach in the entryway. Martha grabbed her hand. "We were worried."

"Did you find Emma?" Uncle Zach asked.

Lizzie shook her head and hurried outside.

She and Caleb climbed into the buggy just as the security guards left Respite Haven and headed to their sedan.

"Give them time to drive away," Caleb told his uncle.

"Did they see you?" Aunt Martha asked.

"They saw Lizzie. Plus, we ran into the manager of Respite Haven. His brother-in-law is Thad Thompson."

"Did you find any information about your friend, Emma?"

"Not today."

Lizzie had found the nursing home where Emma had been kept, but she had arrived too late to find her friend. She was beginning to think she would never find Emma, and that broke her heart.

SEVENTEEN

"I am sorry." Aunt Martha patted Lizzie's hand.

"Mr. Thompson said she was staying at a facility his brother-in-law managed. Suppose she was here but has been moved to another nursing home. If only I could talk to someone who has visited Respite Haven regularly over the last two or three years."

"That would be Trudy Troyer. She never misses. Her husband joins her when he can."

"Is Trudy here today?" Lizzie asked.

"*Yah*." Martha pointed to a plump woman near the hitching rail. "Stay here. I will bring her here so you are not noticed by anyone else."

Martha hurried to talk to her friend and brought her back to the buggy.

"Lizzie is trying to find someone who used to be at the home," Caleb's aunt explained.

Trudy listened as Lizzie provided a description of Emma.

"I am sorry, but so many people come and go here. Plus, my memory is not as good as it used to be." Trudy grabbed Martha's hand and chuckled. "The years take their toll, *yah*?"

"Speak for yourself," Martha replied with a coy smile. "Still, I do not recall all that I used to. Is there anyone else who might remember past residents?"

"Ruben Stoll."

"He lives on Fisher Road?" Martha asked.

Trudy nodded. "You know him. He and his wife had not been married long when she developed cancer. The dear woman died a little over a year ago. He is a hardworking young man and was employed at Respite Haven until a few months ago as an aide. He worked nights and managed his small farm in the daytime. Occasionally he would join us and sing to the residents. He has a magnificent voice."

"He is tall with a sweet smile." Martha nodded. "I remember him."

Caleb leaned closer to his aunt. "Are you saying he might know about former residents?"

"It is worth a try. His farm is not far from here."

"I can take you and Zach home," Trudy suggested. "Let the young folks use your buggy, then they can talk to Ruben without holding you up."

This morning Lizzie had been so sure they would find Emma at Respite Haven. If Ruben Stoll failed to provide further information, Lizzie didn't know where to turn next. She had to find Emma, but she kept running into dead ends that went nowhere.

"Caleb, you and Lizzie must have a sandwich before you leave," Aunt Martha insisted.

But neither of them was hungry. He thanked his

aunt before declining her offer. Working quickly, he transferred the empty cookie tins and basket of sandwiches to the Troyer buggy.

After getting directions to Ruben Stoll's farm, he and Lizzie waved goodbye. Caleb flicked the reins and guided the mare onto the main road.

"We will turn onto a side road soon," Caleb told her. "I will feel relieved once we are on the back roads. The guards could be anywhere."

"Perhaps they are staying in Freemont."

"Which means they could be driving along the main road we are on now."

"At least the stocky guard did not recognize me when he stopped at the refreshment table."

"All Amish look alike, right?" Caleb chuckled. "It seems they see only the clothing, the hat and suspenders for me, the bonnet or *kapp* for women. They lump us together with every other person dressed in *funny* clothing, as they say."

"This is a good thing at the moment."

"*Yah*, it helps to keep you safe."

Caleb tugged on the reins and guided the horse onto the side road. "Let's go, Daisy girl." The mare broke into a brisk trot.

The farmland passed, gentle hills and green pastures. "The land is lovely here, Caleb."

"Different from the mountain. More expansive. Without the rocky terrain, the farmland is rich and productive. I understand why Uncle Zach came here."

"Were they not happy in Ethridge?"

"Aunt Martha has arthritis. The cold winters increased her discomfort so they moved south. The wind is not so sharp and the winter not so long. It was a wise decision. Plus, they like the bishop and the community. They are still committed to the Amish way, but the *Ordnung* is not so stringent in their current church district."

"Some rules are less strict."

"More accepting," Caleb added. "Many of the Amish came here longing for a life that better fit their needs. Uncle Zach said there is more acceptance for those who must work off the farm. Some years the land does not produce enough to feed a large family. It can be hard, and a man must make decisions about how he is to provide for those *Gott* has placed under his care."

Lizzie nodded. "What you are saying makes sense. My father longed for more sons to help him with the farm. His health was not the best. I wonder if he feared not being able to provide for his wife and children."

"The Lord is merciful, but He also demands that we use our intellect and our hands to eke out a living." He looked at the rows of baled hay that would provide feed for the livestock throughout the winter. "Worry can tug at a man's heart even when he puts his trust in *Gott*."

"You are sounding very Amish, Caleb."

"Perhaps you are a good influence."

She smiled sweetly and then asked, "Do you worry about your future?"

He raised a brow. "I do not have a wife and family."

"Yet that will change when we find Emma."

Lizzie had always assumed he and Emma would make a life together without asking what he wanted. Evidently Emma had not confided in Lizzie about the conversation she and Caleb had had before both girls left for the beach. A mix of pain and anger had flashed from Emma's eyes after he had made his pronouncement. As much as he regretted hurting her, he'd needed to be truthful, lest Emma presume there was something more to their friendship.

He thought of his father who jumped to conclusions as well, then flicked the reins again, not willing to dwell on the past. He needed to be totally in the present, to remain vigilant and to keep Lizzie safe.

He glanced around the edge of the buggy, overwhelmed with a foreboding. They were riding in the open with pastures on both sides of the roadway. If the dark sedan appeared, there would be no place to hide.

As much as Caleb admired Lizzie's determination to find their friend, he worried about her disregard for her own well-being. Caleb needed to provide the protection she failed to give herself.

If only he could keep Lizzie safe.

* * *

For all Lizzie's excitement earlier when she'd thought they would find Emma at the nursing home, she was now at a low ebb and wondered if Ruben would provide the information they needed.

Lizzie had been sure Emma was at Respite Haven. Everything had fallen into place with Caleb's relatives knowing the nursing home and the group of Amish volunteers hosting the gathering for the residents. Then to have their search come to naught made her wonder if they would ever find Emma. If only she could go back and erase that day at the beach forever, although mistakes could not be erased and days could not be wiped off the slate of life. Unfortunately.

She had asked *Gott*'s forgiveness, but she also knew that asking was not enough. She had to make restitution for her actions and try to right the wrong, which meant doing everything in her power to find her friend.

Caleb spotted Ruben's farm in the distance. He appeared to own a small tract of land where he raised a few head of cattle, some chickens and goats, probably for milk and cheese. Three horses grazed on a nearby pasture. Bales of hay were neatly stacked to the side of the barn and a few acres of land were covered in winter rye.

A small garden sat to one side of the house.

The exterior was neatly kept and the pastures, fencing and acres were perfectly aligned. Ruben took pride in his property.

"The farm looks lovely," Lizzie said.

Almost at that very moment, a man, not much older than Caleb, stepped from the barn. He was tall and slender with a thick beard and dark black hair that appeared neatly trimmed under his black felt hat.

He eyed both of them with caution.

Caleb pulled the buggy to a stop, then hopped down and approached Ruben with his hand outstretched.

"Caleb Zook. I'm staying with my aunt and uncle. Zachariah and Martha Yoder. They send their regards."

Ruben eyed the outstretched hand and hesitated before he accepted the handshake. "You are not from this area."

"I am originally from Willkommen in the North Georgia mountains."

Lizzie climbed from the buggy and joined Caleb. She nodded a greeting and introduced herself.

"I am looking for a friend who I heard was staying at Respite Haven. We stopped by there earlier with other Amish folks who hosted a gathering for the residents. I could not find my friend and wondered if she has left or moved to another facility."

Ruben stared at both of them but said nothing.

Lizzie glanced at Caleb as if for support before she continued. "Her name is Emma Bontrager. She's a twenty-year-old blond with blue eyes. Do you recall anyone there who fits that description?"

Without comment, Ruben turned and started for his house.

"Sir, please." Lizzie hurried after him. "Do you know anyone at Respite Haven matching that description?"

"I am not at liberty to discuss the residents," he said through tight lips.

"We are not here to do harm, and I would never want you to go against your better judgment, but I am concerned about my friend and am trying to find her."

"Why are you asking me?"

"Trudy Troyer said you worked there for a few years and might remember a young blond resident." She glanced again at Caleb. He nodded his encouragement.

"Sir," she continued. "It is imperative that I find Emma."

"I wish you well in your attempt."

Ruben climbed the stairs of his porch, and with each footfall, Caleb sensed Lizzie's desperation.

"I beg you to give us a few minutes of your time," she pleaded.

Ruben stopped and turned, his mouth drawn

and eyes hooded. "Why should I tell you anything?"

"My friend disappeared three years ago," Lizzie said, the words tumbling out of her mouth. "I believe someone has held her against her will, and I have reason to believe she was held at Respite Haven. Only she is not there, and I do not know where to find her."

Ruben stared at her for a long moment, then he glanced at the distant pasture. Caleb and Lizzie followed his gaze. A gravestone was visible on a small rise.

"Trudy said your wife died. I am sorry for your loss," Lizzie said, as she stepped closer. "Emma was my best friend. We did everything together. She and Caleb planned to marry, but her life was cut short. For so long, we thought she was dead. Then we learned she had been taken, which gave us encouragement. Now we have come to a dead end. You are our only hope."

Ruben stood still for a long moment, as if assessing who they were and whether they were telling the truth. Finally he nodded. "Come inside. I will tell you what I know."

Lizzie gasped with relief. Caleb was taken aback. He had not expected the man's heart to soften. If only Ruben would provide the necessary information that would lead them to Emma.

EIGHTEEN

Talking to Ruben on his porch was one thing, but stepping inside gave Lizzie pause. Neither she nor Caleb knew anything about the man. His first actions had been somewhat off-putting, yet he had seemingly changed direction when she mentioned Emma was in danger.

Following Caleb into the house, she was relieved to find the interior was as neat and tidy as the surrounding farmland.

Ruben motioned them to sit at the kitchen table. "You mentioned a young blond woman with blue eyes."

Lizzie settled into a chair next to Caleb. "Emma Bontrager is her name."

"She sounds like Susanna Jones, although we may be talking about two different people. Susanna came to Respite Haven about three years ago."

Lizzie looked at Caleb. "The timing would be right."

"You were working at Respite Haven then?" Caleb asked.

Ruben nodded, his face heavy. "My wife became infirmed at a very young age. The doctors said she needed physical therapy to stretch her muscles so they would not atrophy. Three times a week, a physical therapist from Respite Haven came to the house. The bills were high. This is not something I wanted to incur onto my neighbors and the good people in my church so I took a job with the nursing home. The physical therapy agency discounted my bill because I worked at the Haven. The community helped somewhat, but the job allowed me to pay for the majority of her care."

"How long ago did your wife die, Ruben?"

"A year and a half ago."

"But you kept working after she passed?" Lizzie asked.

He nodded. "I stayed on mainly because of Susanna. She struggled with her memory, at the onset, and had difficulty with her cognitive function. The nurses said she had been in some type of accident, but she looked as if she had been beaten. I feared she had traumatic brain injury and would never be able to live on her own."

"Yet she improved?" Lizzie asked.

"With time. The cuts healed and the bruises disappeared, although she still walked with a slight limp and her motor skills were not as good as one would hope. I was aware of what the physical therapist had done with my wife after her debilitation, so I worked with Susanna in the evenings over my dinner break."

"You were good to help her," Caleb said.

"Do you know who hurt her?" Ruben asked.

"We have an idea," Lizzie said. "But I fear the

same man may have her now. Do you know anything about a medical symposium Mr. Whitaker might be attending?"

"Does it have something to do with Susanna?"

"I'm not sure. When did she leave Respite Haven?"

Ruben thought for a moment. "Four months ago."

"Do you know why she left?" Caleb asked. "Was it because her memory improved?"

"Perhaps that played a role." Ruben hesitated a moment and then continued. "It may sound strange, but I came to realize Susanna seemed more alert when the head nurse on the evening shift had the day off. Susanna would smile, even laugh at times, and her hands worked more easily."

"You realized this over time?"

"I wish it would have come to me sooner, but I was so rarely with Susanna when the head nurse made her rounds. A few nights, the trays were late coming from the kitchen, and I brought Susanna her dinner when the nurse was there. The pills are dispensed in bubble-wrapped packets so the patient receives exactly what the doctor has prescribed. It is a way to ensure there is not an error in dispensing the meds, yet the nurse gave Susanna a pill from another bottle that was not part of her pill pack."

"And that worried you?"

"Yes, because Susanna was more alert, less lethargic and more mentally sound on the days she went without the extra pill."

"Which coincided with the days the head nurse was absent?" Lizzie asked.

Ruben nodded. "That is correct."

"Could the extra pill have been Tylenol or ibuprofen?" Lizzie asked.

"I know where those bottles are kept. This pill was different."

"Did you mention it to Susanna?"

"I told her to spit out the extra pill after the nurse had left the room."

"What did you determine?"

"As I mentioned, the nights when she did not take the pill, Susanna remained alert. Over time her memory started to return, but she became anxious."

"Because of not taking the pill?"

"Because she could remember some of what had happened to her. The last night I saw her, she grabbed my hand and said she was in danger. I tried to calm her and checked on her before I went home at the end of my shift. By then she was asleep."

He shook his head with regret. "When I returned to work the following day, she was not there. Her things had been moved from her room and there was no sign of her anywhere."

"Did you ask where she had gone?"

"I explained the pill situation to Irene Douglas. She's a caring nurse who shared my concerns. She checked the meds cart but could not find the extra pills. I asked to speak to Mr. Whitaker. He listened and assured me the head nurse was a trusted employee."

"What did he say about Susanna?"

"He said a family member had taken her home to Alabama."

"Did Susanna ever mention family in Alabama?"

"Never. I found it odd that family would take her away in the middle of the night. I questioned the evening and night staff, but no one had seen anything. Her room was at the end of the hallway. A nearby door leads outside. It would be easy enough for a car to be waiting to haul Susanna away."

"Surely a family member would leave a forwarding address."

"I thought of that, as well. I even checked with the pharmacy and the doctor's main office in case they had a forwarding address. No one knew where she had gone."

"You continued working at Respite Haven?"

"Only for a few days. Mr. Whitaker called me in and said he had video footage that showed I was tampering with patient medication. Some oxycodone had gone missing. Mr. Whitaker did not want to call in the police, yet he feared I was involved in something illegal."

"He didn't believe you?"

"Evidently not. He asked me to turn in my resignation, and he said if I did not do so, he would notify law enforcement."

"You did not have a choice."

"I was no longer interested in working if Susanna was not there, yet I was upset that he thought I had done something against the law. It is difficult to have one's reputation impugned, especially in such a way. I have not gone back, although I did learn the evening head nurse moved to Ohio. I have a feeling she was let go, as well."

Ruben raised his hands and shrugged. "Of course, none of this helps you find your friend."

"At least we know Susanna left some time ago. I wish we could be sure she and Emma are the same person."

"Wait here," Ruben said. "I have something to show you."

He climbed the stairs. His footsteps could be heard overhead, and in a few minutes, he returned to the kitchen and held a photograph in his hand.

"The day I realized she was gone, I went to the bulletin board in the lobby. Someone had made a display of photographs taken of the residents. There was one of Susanna. I feared something had happened to her and wanted proof that she had been at Respite Haven."

He stared at the picture and then handed it to Lizzie.

She pulled in a stiff breath. Caleb leaned closer. A number of residents were sitting at a table, chatting with the visitors. Lizzie recognized a few of the people from the gathering today.

After glancing at the various faces in the photo, she came to the woman on the far right. Her mouth went dry. The woman was thin and drawn and her features were pulled, perhaps with worry or a bit of depression or maybe confusion about where she was and what was happening to her.

Lizzie's heart twisted.

The woman in the picture was Emma.

NINETEEN

Caleb worried about Lizzie on the ride home. She was quiet and withdrawn.

"Ruben seems a good man," he offered, hoping to draw her into conversation.

"I'm grateful Trudy Troyer knew of him so we could learn more about Emma. In a way, I'm relieved Andrew was not the reason she was moved from Respite Haven, although I am convinced his uncle knows her whereabouts. Mr. Thompson had mentioned a symposium he and his brother-in-law would attend and asked Andrew not to do anything until after that event. I have a feeling Mr. Thompson wants to make sure he's back in Florida so no one will suspect he's involved."

"Except you know the truth because of what you overheard."

Which is why Estate Security was searching for Lizzie.

"Maybe my aunt and uncle or one of their friends who visit Respite Haven will have an idea where Emma was taken," Caleb suggested.

"But they don't even remember her. From what Thad Thompson said, his brother-in-law was worried because Emma's memory was returning. Perhaps she had mentioned something that made the nurses suspicious. The evening shift should come on at about seven. We could return there and talk to Irene Douglas, the nurse Ruben said he liked. Mr. Whitaker will not be working tonight, and according to Ruben, the nurse who gave Emma extra pills moved back to Ohio."

"But is it wise to go back to the nursing home after Mr. Whitaker asked us to leave?"

"It may not be wise, Caleb, but Irene might have more information about who Susanna left with and where she was taken. If we find Susanna, we will have found Emma."

Much as Caleb didn't want to put Lizzie in danger again, both of them were back in the buggy later that evening, returning to the nursing home.

"Visiting hours probably run until eight or nine o'clock," he told Lizzie. "Let's hope we can find Ruben's friend by then."

There was only one woman at the desk when they entered the east wing. "I'm looking for Irene Douglas," Lizzie said.

"Irene is on break." The woman glanced at her watch. "She should be back in a few minutes. You can wait in the living area."

Caleb didn't like sitting in the main entrance so he guided Lizzie to a smaller side room that appeared to be a library and motioned her to a chair in the corner where she would be hidden from anyone in the hallway.

The five minutes stretched to ten.

Lizzie looked worried.

"We'll wait five more minutes," he said. "If

Irene doesn't show up by then, I think we should leave."

"Ten minutes, Caleb. Let's wait that long."

He paced the floor, his eyes on the hallway, alert to any sign of danger.

Headlights flashed through the front windows, and for a moment, he feared the security guards had returned. Instead, a woman in white scrubs with a coat around her shoulders hurried inside. She carried a book in her hand and headed for the small room where they were waiting.

"Oh, sorry," she said, somewhat startled when she noticed them. "I didn't realize anyone was in the library."

She placed the book on the shelf. "May I help you with something?"

Caleb noticed her name tag. "We've been waiting to see you."

The nurse smiled. "I slipped out during my break to get something at the store."

Lizzie explained talking to Ruben Stoll and his concern about Susanna leaving Respite Haven. "He said you might have information about her whereabouts. She and I were friends a long time ago, and I had hoped to see her again."

"Susanna is a delightful person. I'm sure she would love to see you, as well."

"Did her family transfer her to another facility?"

"I believe Mr. Whitaker made the decision.

He said she needed psychiatric care, although it seemed strange that she was transferred at night. In fact, he transported her in his own car."

"Do you know where he took her?"

"Maybe to Atlanta." The nurse glanced into the hallway, then pulled in a deep breath and lowered her voice. "A nurse left a few months ago, around the time Susanna was moved. She told me Susanna needed to be given Benadryl at night for allergic reactions."

"Did she have allergies?"

"Not that I know of. I think what she called Benadryl was really something more potent."

Once again, she checked the hallway.

"Have you heard of chemical restraint?" she asked. "It's an illegal way some facilities manage their agitated patients."

"You mean giving meds that haven't been prescribed?" Lizzie asked.

Irene nodded. "About a month before she left, Susanna had started to get agitated at night. Ruben had noticed it. I did, as well. She said some strange things at times. I had told the night nurse, although I regret doing so now. Susanna confided in me that she was afraid and had asked for help."

"Did she say what she was afraid of?"

"Nothing surfaced. She had traumatic brain injury or so it said on her chart, yet she didn't struggle to put words together or express her thoughts. In my opinion, she appeared to have amnesia."

"Did you mention that to anyone?"

"I told the other nurse. She brushed off my concerns. I probably shouldn't be talking to you tonight, but it's been troubling me ever since."

Irene glanced at her watch. "I need to get back to work. Can I call you if I uncover anything else?"

"Tell Ruben if you see him," Caleb said.

"I go by his house on my way home from work. Will he know how to get in touch with you?"

"He knows some distant relatives who will get the message to us. We're grateful for your help."

As soon as the woman left the library, Caleb and Lizzie hurried outside. He helped her into the buggy and encouraged Daisy into a brisk trot. Caleb wanted to get on the back road as quickly as possible.

The night was cold, and he regretted returning to Respite Haven. They had learned nothing new except that Mr. Whitaker had probably arranged for Emma to be given Benadryl—or something more potent—at night and that he had moved her in his own private vehicle.

Where had he taken her and why?

Lizzie tried to put the pieces together as the clip-clop of the mare's hooves sounded on the pavement. The air was cool, and she pulled a blanket over their legs.

"I'm fine," Caleb said, but she knew he was cold. She also knew he was worried. She could tell by the tension that emanated from him and the way he kept glancing at the road behind them.

"We're okay," he said as if sensing her upset and trying to reassure her. "No one will see us."

Except she was tired and nervous. The day had been long but had started off so promising. Foolishly she had thought they would find Emma. Now they were even more confused about where she was. Instead of getting closer to finding her, she was slipping through their fingers.

"Where did Mr. Whitaker take her?" Lizzie mused aloud.

"If only we could ask him."

She nodded. "Yet that would set off all types of warning buzzers. I'm afraid his brother-in-law's security men would be at Respite Haven before we could ask the questions we need answered. I'm already worried we've said too much to too many people. I trust Ruben, but I'm not sure about Irene. She seemed nice enough and shared information, yet a woman who talks so easily could divulge information about two people asking questions."

"I hope she won't tell Mr. Whitaker about our late night visit. To be safe, I want you to stay close to the house tomorrow. We'll both keep our eyes on the road and make certain no one driving by the farm spots either of us.

"I'll help your aunt. She said she has much to do."

"And I'll work on the farm, but I'll be watching for a dark sedan with tinted windows."

Headlights appeared in the distance, heading in their direction. Caleb nudged Lizzie. "Climb in the back of the buggy."

"What?"

He pointed to the approaching car. "I don't want your face captured in the headlights of oncoming traffic. Hurry."

She climbed into the rear and slumped down in the seat, her heart pounding. "Can you tell who it is?"

"Probably someone leaving town, but I don't know where they are going this time of night."

The lights nearly blinded Caleb. He held his hand in front of his eyes to shield them from the glare.

The car raced past.

"Did you see the color of the vehicle?" she asked.

"It looked black, but at night it's hard to tell."

What wasn't hard to tell, as she peered through the small opening at the rear of the buggy, was that the car had pulled into the nursing home parking lot and was turning around. It angled back onto the main road and accelerated.

Her pulse raced. "Caleb, they're coming after us."

"Hold on." He flicked the reins. Daisy picked up her pace. "There's a turnoff, but I don't know if we'll make it in time."

How could the turnoff offer protection with the expanse of farmland on each side of the road? She glanced back again, her stomach churning. The sedan was racing toward them.

"We've got to get over the next hill," Caleb shouted to her.

She held onto the rear seat and strained to see the hill in the distance. Daisy was racing full speed along the road, but the mare couldn't outrun the car that was steadily gaining on them.

"Oh, Caleb," Lizzie moaned, hating the fear that clutched at her heart.

A truck crested the hill on the opposite side of the road. A horn bellowed a warning.

"Come on, girl," Caleb encouraged his mare.

"Why's the trucker blowing his horn?" Lizzie glanced over her shoulder. The sedan was straddling the median and driving in the middle of the road.

"They're trying to pass us," Caleb yelled.

Again, the truck's horn bellowed.

Lizzie held her breath, anticipating the impending crash of the two motor vehicles. At the last possible minute, the sedan pulled back into the right-hand lane just before the truck raced past.

The sedan shimmied and deaccelerated, giving Lizzie a moment of hope.

The crest of the hill lay just ahead.

"Just a little farther, Daisy." Caleb's voice cut through the night.

The mare responded to his prodding. As if gaining a new burst of energy, Daisy galloped over the hill.

On the far side, the road split.

Caleb bypassed the turn to the right and continued on the main road.

Lizzie's stomach rolled. She had expected him to turn right onto the road that led to his aunt and uncle's farm. "What are you doing, Caleb?"

"Finding a place to hide. An Amish couple has a small farm on the left. The path angles away from the road and is flanked by tall pines and hardwoods. It's at the next bend in the road."

From the tension in Caleb's shoulders, he appeared as worried as Lizzie was.

The main road curved right. He slowed the mare and made a fast left-hand turn. Almost too fast. The wheels came up as the mare hurried onto a dirt path, nearly obscured by thick vegetation.

Caleb pulled on the reins and angled the buggy into a small clearing that was hidden from the road.

"Easy, Daisy. Stay still, girl."

They both glanced back. The car that had been

following them crested the hill and then veered right onto the back road that led to Ruben's house and eventually to his aunt and uncle's farm.

Perhaps the guards knew where she and Caleb were staying.

"They've driven out of sight," Lizzie gasped, trying to catch her breath. Although relieved, she knew they were still in danger. "What do we do now?"

"We wait."

"Wait?"

"They'll be back."

Caleb's voice made her shiver. She glanced over her shoulder and watched the country road as time passed ever so slowly. The darkness was unsettling, and she blinked to ensure she wasn't imagining someone crawling through the woods. They would be hard-pressed to escape, especially if the men had weapons.

The night air turned cold, and she longed for the protection of Aunt Martha's kitchen or the warmth of Caleb's arms.

An owl hooted. Lizzie flinched. "I don't like this, Caleb." They were sitting like ducks on a pond with hunters circling the water.

Suddenly lights appeared.

He raised a finger to his lips. "Shh. Remain silent."

She said nothing and both of them listened to the sound of the motor as the car backtracked to the main road. It turned right and then accelerated. Tires screeched, and no doubt, rubber would be visible on the pavement in the morning.

The guards had taken the country road, expecting to follow a buggy. Eventually they had given up their search, turned round and were headed back to town, never seeing the small unpaved path into the woods where Caleb and Lizzie were hiding.

Caleb expressed what they both knew to be true. "If not for the secluded path, they would have stopped us on the road."

Lizzie dared not think of what could have happened to both of them.

Aunt Martha and Uncle Zach were waiting for them when they returned home. "We were worried," his aunt said. "Is everything all right?"

"We had to wait for the nurse to come back from her dinner break, which delayed us."

"Did you find any information?" she asked.

"Only that Emma is not there now. Where she is, we have no idea."

"You will find her," Aunt Martha encouraged.

Lizzie was not so sure. She looked at Caleb's drawn face and knew he felt the same as she did.

They had left Pinecraft in hopes of finding Emma. Now she realized they might never see Emma again.

TWENTY

Lizzie couldn't sleep. She kept seeing Emma being taken away in a dark sedan with tinted windows. Taken where? Lizzie didn't know. Tears came in the night. She cried for everything that had happened and because nothing was going right. Eventually she cried herself to sleep, and when she awoke the next morning, her head pounded and she felt achy all over.

"Could it be the flu?" Aunt Martha asked when Lizzie entered the kitchen and explained her symptoms. The sweet older woman placed her hand on Lizzie's forehead. "You do not seem feverish. Still, I can see in your eyes that you are not feeling well."

From crying most of the night. Lizzie failed to share how unsettled she had been.

"I presume Caleb has been up for hours," she said.

"Not quite that long, but the men started working before dawn. Caleb is such a help. Without children of our own, it brings more hardship on Zachariah. I worry he gets too tired. He does not complain, but I can see his fatigue when he comes in at night. Most times, I must call him to eat or he would stay outside working until well after dark."

Lizzie thought of her brothers who helped her

father. She had believed he loved the boys more, but perhaps her practical father, who was devoted to the land, was thinking more about his farm than playing favorites with his children.

"Are you all right, dear?" Aunt Martha was staring at her.

"I was thinking of my own father. I never understood the attention he paid to my brothers. After what you said, I wonder if I was thinking of my own sense of inadequacy instead of my father's needs."

"Some men cannot relate to women. They do not understand how we think and act and react to various situations. Especially those men who did not have sisters."

"My father had three brothers," Lizzie shared.

Martha patted her hand. "You were a blessing to your family, of this I am certain."

At the moment, Lizzie felt like a self-absorbed child who saw the world through her own gaze instead of thinking of others.

She had thought she was doing the right thing finding Emma but in so doing, she had turned her back on her family. Perhaps when all this was over, Lizzie should return to Willkommen. She needed to talk to her *datt*, even if he did not want to hear what she had to say. She needed to apologize for the way she had misjudged him. She also needed to ensure her *mamm* understood why she had left—not because of her mother but due to Lizzie's own need to make right what she had put into play three years ago.

"Sit, dear." Aunt Martha's voice was soothing. She rubbed her hand over Lizzie shoulder and ushered her to the table.

"I will pour you a cup of coffee, unless you wish to go back to bed."

"No, I am acting childish, Aunt Martha, and you are too good to me. Here I have come into your life and brought problems."

"But *you* are not a problem, dear. Plus, you have brought Caleb back to us. He is like the son we never had. His mother and I were close growing up. I regret not seeing her, but having you and Caleb here brings joy to my heart."

Martha's kindness only made Lizzie want to cry more. Contrasting her own self-centeredness to Aunt Martha's goodness and warm acceptance made Lizzie even more upset with herself.

"You are worried about your friend, perhaps?"

Lizzie nodded. "She has moved from Respite Haven and we do not know where she has been taken."

"What about Ruben?"

"He is as flummoxed as we are."

"There was talk among the Amish community that he was taken with the young woman because of the hole in his heart after his wife died. The woman at the nursing home filled a need in his loneliness. I am sure he helped her, as well. At that time, no one realized she was Amish. The woman herself, as I understand, had no memory of her faith."

"Emma was and is Amish, although she has lived another life—evidently a very confused life—at Respite Haven. How could anyone hold a person captive for so long? My heart breaks thinking about what Emma has had to endure."

All because of me, Lizzie thought.

"It is because of your compassion that you have searched for her."

"My actions are not to be applauded, Aunt Martha. I could not forget her when her need was always on my mind."

"Sometimes *Gott* places people in our hearts who need prayer or help. We do not always realize from where those promptings come, but I am convinced they come from *Gott*."

If Aunt Martha was right, then the Lord had been encouraging Lizzie all this time to find Emma. If so, why had He allowed the trail to go cold?

Martha poured a cup of coffee and placed it on the table. "You are staying up, dear?"

"What can I do to help you?"

"I planned to make noodles for the meal, along with mashed potatoes. I have a pot roast in the icehouse. Soon, Zachariah will go to town for more ice. Lugging the heavy bags from the wagon is hard work. My husband does not complain, yet I know his back troubles him after such intense labor."

"Perhaps Caleb will stay with you for a few months, Aunt Martha. If so, he could help Uncle Zach."

"That would bring joy to our hearts, but what of you, dear?"

Lizzie raised the mug to her lips and took a sip of the hot brew. "I'll need to return home. My parents do not know where I am."

"You did not tell them?"

"I told my mother I had to find Emma, but she doesn't know where I am."

"You could write her. I have paper and pen. Receiving mail from you would alleviate her worry."

Why hadn't she thought of that herself?

"Write home first," Martha said. "Then we will tend to the noodles, *yah*?"

She pulled a tablet and envelope from a drawer and placed it on the table in front of Lizzie, along with a ballpoint pen.

"Would you like something to eat, dear?"

"Not now. I will write my letter and then help you. The hard task needs to be done first."

Aunt Martha patted Lizzie's shoulder. "I will leave you alone to gather your thoughts, while I tend to more jobs upstairs. Let me know when you are finished. I have stamps, and we will leave your letter in the box by the road for the mailman."

Lizzie took another sip of coffee and then lifted the pen into her hands.

Dear Mamm and Datt...

There was so much to tell—most of all, she needed to ask forgiveness. The words started to flow and with them a bit of healing. Her parents could either accept her apology and welcome her back or ignore her letter.

Only time would tell.

After dinner that night, Lizzie did the dishes, wiped them dry and returned them to the cupboard, while Martha tended to some mending. She and Uncle Zach sat near the wood stove in the main room. He read the paper, the same one where Lizzie's photograph had appeared. Caleb had gone outside and taken a lantern.

Lizzie could see the soft glow from the oil lamp through the window. She wiped her hands and hung the dish towel over the hook by the sink.

"I will take Caleb a fresh cup of coffee," she told his relatives as she filled a mug.

The moon peered from between the clouds and covered the barnyard with a peaceful glow.

Lizzie wrapped her cape around her shoulders and hurried to where Caleb sat. She saw the whittling knife in his hand and the shavings on the ground at his feet. Stepping closer, she placed the cup on a nearby stump.

"Thank you, Lizzie. You read my mind about

the coffee." He offered her a grateful smile as he lifted the mug and took a long swig of the hot brew.

"What are you carving?"

"Something I started night before last."

She peered at the block of wood, unable to discern what he was creating in the half-light.

A stiff breeze swirled around them, and she hugged her arms to ward off the chill. "It is a cold night to be outside."

"*Yah*, but I needed to think and this is how my mind clears away the problems of the day."

"You're thinking about how we will find Emma?" she asked.

He nodded. "The fact that she was moved from Respite Haven concerns me, especially since we have no clue to her whereabouts."

Caleb set the mug down and returned to his whittling, his hands sure and quick with the wood. His expression intensified as he worked and he seemed totally absorbed in the task. Every so often, he would rub his fingers over the piece as if rubbing life into the wood.

Lizzie watched him for a long moment, enthralled by the details that started to form, before asking, "Do you see the object you are carving before it takes shape?"

He raised a brow as if unsure of her question.

"When I watch you whittle," she continued, "it seems as if you see something that is not there yet. Something in the wood that you are trying to reveal."

He stared at her in the muted half-light. "You are an insightful woman, Lizzie."

Her pulse quickened, and she took a step back, unsure how to respond to the sincerity of his tone.

"My family did not understand," he said, his voice heavy laden. "They had lived with me my whole life. You and I have been apart for three years, and yet, you express exactly what is in my heart."

"I'm sure Emma understood, as well."

He shook his head. "You think more of Emma than you do yourself."

"I don't understand?"

"Emma was centered on Emma."

"Oh, Caleb, don't say such things. Emma's heart was in the right place."

"Perhaps." He held up the project he was carving. "Tell me what you see in the wood."

"I see angles and plains that could be anything, but in your hands they will develop into something beautiful. This is a part of who you are, as if you and the wood come together as you carve. It is your gift."

"A gift my father could not accept."

"Aunt Martha said the Lord prompts us to do things. He prompts you to carve and to create delightful objects with your hands and your knives. *Yah*, this is a special gift given only to a few. No matter what your *datt* thinks, you must accept that gift and use it to touch the hearts of others."

He stared at the wood. "How can an object touch another's heart?"

"By the beauty it brings and the specialness of your creation. You are creating something where before there was only a piece of wood. You breathe life into it, Caleb."

He placed the wood next to the coffee cup and stood.

"Is something wrong?" she asked.

"Thank you, Lizzie."

She tilted her head, confused by his comment.

He stepped closer.

Even with the night swirling around them, she could see something in his eyes not there before, something that made her insides feel like gelatin. Her pulse raced and she wanted to stay captured in his gaze.

"Lizzie, I—"

He rubbed his finger along her cheek, his touch gentle. She leaned into him. He slipped his hand around her neck. A tingle of excitement curled along her spine.

The moon peered from the cloud-covered sky and cast a ribbon of light over Caleb's face. He stared into her eyes.

The pit of her stomach tightened. More than anything, she wanted to weave her fingers through his hair.

His eyes narrowed, but she saw no ill will. Instead, she saw a warmth that moved her heart.

"Lizzie," he whispered. The huskiness in his voice touched her to the core.

She lifted her head. A portion of her melted as he wrapped her more deeply in his embrace.

The only thing she could see were his lips as he lowered them to hers.

For one beautiful moment, the world stood still, and she was transported to some ethereal place filled with warmth and love and emotion. She molded into his arms, longing for the kiss to continue forever.

SNAP! A twig broke.

She jerked back, started by the sound. Someone was nearby.

Concern flashed from Caleb's eyes. He raised his finger to his lips. "Shh."

He stepped protectively in front of her.

"Who's there?" he demanded.

No answer.

He motioned her at the side of the barn. "Stay in the shadows," he whispered before rounding the barn.

She heard nothing, except his footfalls. When they stilled, her heart raced even more, fearing for his safety.

"Caleb," she said, her voice low. The memory of his kiss was still on her lips, but her heart pulsed with another terrifying thought.

Where was Caleb? What had happened to him?

TWENTY-ONE

Still flushed from Lizzie's kiss, Caleb stood perfectly still, hoping to discover what was waiting for him in the darkness. Bobcats and coyotes sometimes prowled the area. Foxes were frequently seen, yet he had not thought of an animal when the twig snapped. He had thought immediately of a human being.

The moon peered out from behind the clouds.

He saw nothing, which made him even more concerned.

Make yourself known, he said inwardly, his gaze steady on the landscape.

"Caleb?"

Lizzie peered around the barn.

"Stay back."

"Maybe it was the wind."

He didn't think so, but he needed to protect Lizzie and get her into the house. "Come, Lizzie. You must go inside."

He hurried her into the kitchen. His aunt and uncle had gone upstairs and had left the oil lamps burning in the kitchen.

"Keep away from the windows." He turned down the lamps. "Don't come outside unless I tell you everything is okay."

"But—"

"For your safety. For my aunt and uncle's safety, as well."

She nodded. "Stay on the porch, Caleb. Don't go into the barn area."

He squeezed her hand. "I appreciate your concern." Stepping outside, he closed the door behind him, then glanced through the window, waiting for Lizzie to flip the lock.

She stepped forward, glared at him as if upset that he had put himself in danger and applied the lock.

Letting out a relieved breath, he stared again into the darkness. If someone was out there, they would be waiting for him. He would wait, as well.

The moon went behind the clouds and darkness settled over the farmland. He stepped deeper into the shadows.

Another twig snapped. Whoever or whatever was there was drawing closer.

Caleb left the porch and again neared the barn.

A large form raised up in front of him. His pulse raced. He lunged, wrapped his arms around the creature and flung it to the ground.

Not an animal but a man.

He pushed his arms against the guy's shoulders and held him down. "Who are you and what are you doing here?"

"Let me go."

"Not until you—"

He recognized the voice and let up on his hold ever so slightly.

The clouds drifted and moonlight spilled over the man's face. "Ruben? What's going on?"

"I… I did not want to wake up your aunt and uncle."

"You nearly got yourself hurt."

Caleb climbed to his feet and offered Ruben a hand up. "I want to trust you, Ruben, so start talking and talk fast. I do not like people who sneak around at night. Explain why you are here."

"I went to Warm Springs."

"The town on the way to Atlanta?"

"*Yah.* I heard they had job openings at the large rehab center there. If Whitaker thought Susanna needed psychiatric help, he might have taken her there."

Caleb nodded. Ruben had his attention and his interest. "What did you find?"

"I filled out a job application, then I asked to look around. The receptionist gave me a tour. Everyone there is proud of their facility and eager to spread the news of what they are doing."

"But you were looking for Susanna?"

"I was. The receptionist took me through the orthopedic area. They do a lot of work with prosthetics and also with latent polio victims."

"Susanna didn't have polio."

"But she had problems with her leg. The receptionist was called back to her office. She thought

I would leave when she did, but I strolled around by myself and showed Susanna's photograph to a number of the workers. No one recognized her."

"So why did you come here tonight?"

"Lizzie mentioned a medical symposium. I saw signs announcing the event. It will take place at the rehab center."

"Isn't President Roosevelt's Little White House in Warm Springs?"

"*Yah*, and I learned more about his interest in the town from the receptionist. As you may know, Roosevelt came to Georgia after he was paralyzed with polio to bathe in the hot mineral springs. He felt some relief and eventually founded the rehab center for other polio victims."

Caleb nodded. "I remember reading articles about the therapeutic pools. As I recall there was a chapel on the grounds where he attended services, as well as homes where the families stayed who had children receiving treatments."

"This is true. The small cottages and chapel are situated on the grounds of the center. He built a house for himself nearby and visited often while he was president, which is why it was called the Little White House."

"What about the symposium?"

"This is what I wanted to tell Lizzie. It will start Friday and run through Saturday morning."

"So Mr. Thompson will be in town and Andrew might be, as well."

"Again, I am sorry to upset you," Ruben said. "I was not sure if this was the right farm. At first, I thought someone else lived here. I tried to see if a name was on the house, but I could not see anything in the dark."

"It's okay, Ruben. Come inside. Lizzie will want to hear what you learned."

She opened the door as they neared the house. "Ruben, why were you hiding from us?"

Caleb explained what Ruben had found out.

"Warm Springs? Is that where they're holding Emma?"

"I did not see her, nor did I find anyone with that name," Ruben said. "Yet it makes sense that they would take her to a facility where Mr. Thompson and Mr. Whitaker planned to be."

"That's why Thompson told Andrew not to do anything until after the symposium. He did not want anyone to think he was involved."

Lizzie shook her head with regret. "He doesn't care about his son's well-being or about a poor defenseless woman. All he cares about is his reputation so he can run for office. He's a heartless man."

She looked at Caleb. "We have to go to Warm Springs. I want to see the area and any care facilities where Emma might be held."

He shook his head. "It's not safe, Lizzie."

"Maybe not, but we don't have a choice. Time is running out, and I'm determined to find her."

"Jeb Grayson might have more information," Caleb mentioned. "I wish we had a way to contact him. If he calls my old number, he'll never reach me."

"Perhaps I can help." Ruben pulled a mobile device from his pocket and handed it to Caleb. "I needed a cell phone when I worked at the nursing home and had it with me today in case the rehab center called about my application. Phone your friend."

"Thanks, Ruben. Jeb's a journalist who's been covering the Thompson family." Caleb tapped in a number and raised the phone to his ear.

"It's ringing."

Lizzie pulled in a deep breath. "Would you like a cup of coffee, Ruben, while we wait?"

He shook his head. "I am fine, but *danki*. And I am sorry to cause problems tonight. It is late, yet I wanted you to know about the symposium."

"What type of job did you apply for?" she asked.

"I asked to be considered for an aide position, although I will take anything. I need to get into the rehab center to see if Susanna is there."

"Are there other facilities where she could have been taken?"

"Warm Springs is the closest."

Jeb's number went to voice mail. Caleb left his name and then pushed the phone closer to his ear. "The symposium for long-term care facilities will be held in Warm Springs. I'm not sure if you were aware of the location. If you can, call this number and leave a message. The owner of the phone will contact me."

Caleb disconnected and handed the phone to Ruben. "Let me know if he calls you back."

"*Yah*, for sure."

He stood as if to leave when his phone rang. Ruben looked at the monitor. "Unknown caller. It might be your friend." He handed the cell to Caleb.

Caleb accepted the call and smiled when he heard Jeb's voice.

"It's good to hear from you," the reporter said. "I tried calling your cell a number of times without success."

"That's because I discarded the phone." Caleb nodded to Lizzie. "Did you hear about the symposium in Warm Springs?"

"Harold Fraser, the AJC reporter I told you about, contacted me. He's there now. I'll arrive Friday morning."

"You'll be in Warm Springs?"

"That's right. I'm staying at the Hotel Warm Springs."

"We'll try to get to town that day, as well."

A low-battery notice appeared on the phone monitor. "Listen, Jeb. The phone's losing its charge."

"Stop by the hotel on Friday, if you have time.

We can compare notes on what we've learned about Thompson. Did you find your friend?"

"Not yet. We're hoping she might be at the rehab center."

"That would be convenient."

Caleb had to agree. As soon as the senior Thompson left the area, Andrew could arrange for Emma to disappear or have an accident or come down with some medical emergency that would claim her life.

"How long are you staying in Warm Springs?" Caleb asked.

"Until after the symposium on Saturday. Harold plans to interview the speakers. Bottom line, he wants to end Thad Thompson's run for Congress and expose him as the criminal he really is. I'm still focused on Andrew and what he's been doing to young women who get in his way."

"They both need to be in jail."

"Agreed! I don't have to tell you Thompson is a hateful man who will do anything to maintain his reputation and keep his criminal activity buried. Be careful isn't strong enough. Stay out of his clutches. And tell that girlfriend of yours to watch herself. Andrew has always been attracted to dark-haired beauties."

"Emma has blond hair," Caleb countered.

"Which struck me strange when your girlfriend described her. Andrew never liked blondes. He said they couldn't be trusted. All the women with whom he's had a relationship have had dark hair.'

"What about the island girls who went missing?"

"The same. Dark hair, brown eyes. He hasn't changed him MO in all the years I've been looking into his nefarious activities."

Caleb disconnected and stared at Lizzie, who was talking to Ruben.

Lizzie had dark hair and brown eyes. If what Jeb said was true, Lizzie was the type of person Andrew would have gone after. Not Emma.

Something didn't add up.

He trusted Lizzie. Or at least he had in the past. Now, he wondered if he had misplaced his trust. Was she being truthful about what had happened on the beach, or had she changed her story to suit her own needs?

TWENTY-TWO

"I thought I heard someone in the house last night," Aunt Martha said the next morning as she and Lizzie were doing the wash. The day was cold with a brisk breeze but laundry needed to be done even on chilly days when the sun did not shine.

The wringer washing machine was set up in an outbuilding. Uncle Zach had attached a diesel motor to run the agitation cycle once the tub was filled with water. After the first load of clothing had been washed, Lizzie fed the items through the hand-cranked wringer to remove the water.

Working together, the women emptied the wash water, refilled the tub and repeated the agitation cycle, this time to rinse the clothing before Lizzie fed them through the wringer a second time.

Clothes lines were strung at the side of the house, but with today's overcast skies, Aunt Martha decided to hang the clothing on the porch in case of rain. Nothing was worse than having nearly dry laundry soaked by an unexpected shower.

Lizzie's hands were chaffed and cold by the time they finished rinsing the first three loads.

"Washing is a better job in the summer, *yah*?" Aunt Martha said. She rubbed her hands together.

"Your hands are hurting." Lizzie noticed Martha's drawn face.

"A bit of arthritis from the cold water. It will pass."

"Let me rinse the last load while you go into the kitchen and pour a hot cup of coffee. Holding the warm mug might help your hands."

"You are a thoughtful woman," Martha said with a smile. "Usually I would not accept your offer, but today my joints are swollen and the pain is intense."

"I'm sorry for your discomfort."

"It is what it is," she said with a shrug. "Are you sure you can manage the machine?"

"It is not a problem."

"Caleb and Zachariah are mucking the stalls. They should be finished about the time you get the wash on the line. We will eat when all of you come inside."

"Take care of your hands first. I can help with the meal when I finish here."

After Martha hurried back to the house, Lizzie rinsed the final load, fed the clothing through the wringer and placed them in the clothes basket.

She was ready to empty the final tub of rinse water when a car turned into the drive. Concerned about who would be visiting, she moved to the window and peered outside.

A deputy sheriff's car braked to a stop by the back porch.

Lizzie's pulse quickened.

As the deputy exited his car, Aunt Martha stepped out of the house and stared at him from the porch. The expression on her face was anything but welcoming.

Lizzie moved closer to the open doorway in hopes of hearing what the deputy had to say.

"Have you seen anyone who looks like this?" The deputy climbed the porch steps and held up his cell phone for Martha to see.

She glanced at the outbuilding and then back at the picture. "This woman is *Englisch*?"

"She grew up Amish, but she left the Amish community and traveled to Pinecraft, Florida."

"*Ach*! Pinecraft is far from here."

"Have you seen her, ma'am?"

"Why do you ask?"

"Someone said the woman was at Respite Haven yesterday. They thought she had arrived in your buggy."

"We did not give an *Englisch* woman a ride yesterday."

"She could have been dressed Amish," he added.

"Yet this does not make sense."

The deputy sighed. "Ma'am, you understand what I'm saying."

"I am confused, for sure."

"Could I speak to your husband?"

"He is in one of the nearby pastures, although I do not know where exactly."

The deputy glanced at the surrounding farm-land.

Lizzie's heart thumped. Caleb and his uncle were in the barn and probably unaware of the deputy's presence.

"Mind if I look around, ma'am?"

"This is not something my husband would agree for you to do."

"Ma'am, I do not want any harm to come to you or your husband. We are trying to locate a phone registered to Miss Elizabeth Kauffman and a second mobile registered to a man by the name of Caleb Zook. They both lived originally in the North Georgia mountains."

"I believe you are confused about them being Amish. The Amish do not use phones, even cell phones."

He nodded. "I understand, ma'am, but I doubt there could be two Caleb Zooks. It is an unusual name."

"The name is common among the Amish. There is a John Zook, who lives in the next county. Eli Zook has a farm not far from here, and Abraham Zook is newly married and living with his wife closer to Freemont. Perhaps you want to talk to those Zooks."

The deputy looked confused. Lizzie was glad

Aunt Martha was standing her ground and not letting the deputy intimidate her.

Uncle Zach stepped from the barn. He shook hands with the deputy and introduced himself. "How may I help you?"

The deputy repeated what he had told Aunt Martha.

"I do not know about people who are not Amish but dress Amish. Perhaps you would like a piece of pie and a cup of coffee."

Uncle Zach glanced at his wife. "Right, Martha? You have pie?"

The deputy held up his hand. "I have other houses to visit."

"Then you will take a pie with you." Uncle Zach smiled at his wife with encouragement. "We have a pie to give this fine young man."

She harrumphed and did not seem eager to part with her pastry.

"Martha, he is working hard to keep the area safe. His work should be rewarded." Uncle Zach raised his brow and Aunt Martha seemed to finally understand.

"I would be happy to prepare a pie for you to take home." She hurried into the house and returned minutes later with a pie in hand.

"You have a wife?" she asked, handing him the wrapped pastry.

The deputy blushed. "No, ma'am, not yet."

"A girlfriend?"

He shook his head again.

"You live with your parents?"

"I do."

"They will enjoy the pie."

"Thank you, ma'am, I'm sure they will. And I'm sorry to have bothered you."

"I think this woman you are looking for is on a bus going someplace far away, Deputy. You should not worry about her. If she is not living Amish, then she is not here in the area."

"That's good to hear, ma'am."

Caleb slipped into the washhouse and whispered to Lizzie. "What's the deputy want?"

"He's looking for a woman who was Amish and has been living *Englisch* in Pinecraft. Also a man whose cell phone ended up someplace."

"Since when did the sheriff's office get involved?"

She shrugged. "Mr. Thompson is coming to town. Perhaps law enforcement wants to make sure nothing happens to him."

"You are probably right."

Lizzie nodded. "Your aunt handled him well. She never said I was not here, but she made it seem as if she did not know me."

"Aunt Martha is a shrewd woman."

"And your uncle is sending him home with a pie. He has made a friend instead of an enemy."

"Bless both of them for their ability to make something good out of a difficult situation."

The deputy climbed into his sedan, waved and then pulled out of the drive and onto the main road, heading back to town.

Aunt Martha and Uncle Zach rushed into the washhouse. "You're being sought by the sheriff's office," Zach said, his voice and face tight with worry.

"Lizzie, you must be careful," Martha warned. "I will handle the laundry while you go inside. The deputy is stopping at other houses in the area, and I do not want him to drive by again and wonder about the young woman hanging clothing to dry when I said it was just my husband and myself."

"I'm sorry, Aunt Martha. I'm causing both of you problems."

"Why is this Mr. Thompson so influential?" Uncle Zach asked.

"He has money," Caleb volunteered. "And he has the ear of the police in Sarasota. They must have called law-enforcement departments in this area as they try to find Lizzie. Now they think she is Amish. Before they thought she was *Englisch*."

"And they mentioned your phone, Caleb. What happened to it?"

He chuckled. "I asked an Amish man on the bus to destroy both phones with a hammer and toss them into his manure pit. I doubt law enforcement would be able to track them there."

As they laughed, Lizzie stared at the road through the window. She was worried about finding Emma. Now she was worried about the sheriff's office finding her.

She could not bring danger to Caleb's aunt and uncle. She had to leave and leave soon so that no harm came to them. They were wonderful people who did not deserve anything negative to happen.

If she had realized what would befall them, she would have rejected Caleb's offer to help, but then where would she be and what would have happened to her?

Caleb knew something was wrong with Lizzie. She had said little since the deputy had stopped by the house. She appeared worried and kept looking out the window at the road. Twice a car had driven by the house and she had frozen in place, her hands clutching the kitchen counter and her eyes wide with worry.

She and Aunt Martha had squabbled over who would hang the laundry until it was decided the clothing could be hung in the washhouse so no one from the road would see Lizzie as she worked. They opened the windows to allow the fresh air to circulate before both women returned to the kitchen.

Lizzie remained inside for the rest of the day and insisted Caleb work in the barn but not in the pasture. His uncle had jobs in the barn that needed to be done, hay to move and gear to be saddle-soaped, all of which took Caleb most of the day.

That night after dinner, his aunt and uncle went upstairs early as if they too were unsettled by the visitor and fatigued by the tension that hung heavy in the air.

Lizzie heated water and made a pot of tea. Caleb joined her at the kitchen table. "You have to calm down," he told her.

"How can I after the deputy was here looking for me? If he was looking for me, others are, as well. Perhaps I should go back to Willkommen."

"You do not mean that."

"In a way I do, especially if we do not find Emma. Although first I want to go to Warm Springs and search for her myself. While there, we can talk to Jeb. He might know something that will help us find her."

"We'll head there in the morning as you mentioned."

She glanced down at her dress and apron. "They are looking for me within the Amish community. I need to dress *Englisch* and you do as well, Caleb, and we need transportation."

"My uncle has an extra buggy we can use."

She rolled her eyes. "When do the *Englisch* drive buggies?"

"Never." He smiled. "But an automobile will be difficult to come by."

"Some farmers buy old cars for their sons when they are in *rumspringa*. You know how boys long to drive." Her eyes twinkled. "I remember when you drove Levi Beiler's car."

Caleb chuckled at the memory. "And almost ran off the road the first time I was behind the wheel, but you are right. There could be a farmer who has an old car parked in his barn. My uncle will know this."

"Once we have a car, we can go to town and meet Jeb."

Caleb reached for her hand. "Lizzie, about last night—"

"It is in the past."

She stepped around him, placed her cup and saucer in the sink and hurried upstairs, leaving him with a heaviness in his heart.

The next morning, Caleb and Lizzie talked to his aunt and uncle about their plan.

Aunt Martha patted Lizzie's hand. "I do not like you being on your own when the police are looking for you, dear."

"Caleb will be with me. We will be safe."

"I am not sure."

Nor was Caleb, although they needed to talk to Jeb. He was meeting the AJC reporter and both of them might have information that could help Lizzie and Caleb find Emma.

"Promise me you will be careful," Aunt Martha said. "Do nothing that could cause you harm. And let us know what is happening."

"Ruben has a phone he uses when he works as an aide. We will call him if there is anything you need to know. He will ensure you get the message."

"I do not like this," Uncle Zach said.

Neither did Caleb, but it was their only option if they wanted to find Emma.

"Does old man Jeffries still have that car in his barn?" Caleb asked.

Uncle Zach nodded. "He refused to sell it, yet it costs him money to buy insurance and to keep it running. He abides by the *Ordnung*, except for the car that is a source of pride and something with which he cannot part."

"Do you think he would allow me to drive his car to Warm Springs?"

"Jeffries is thrifty to a fault. If you ask to rent the vehicle and offer enough money, he might agree."

In order to get to town in a timely manner, Caleb and Lizzie needed a car. Mr. Jeffries's vehicle was their only option. If they couldn't save Emma, it would be their last option.

TWENTY-THREE

Lizzie stayed with Aunt Martha as Caleb and his uncle left in the buggy. She helped Martha with the bread baking, but her mind was on the car and how they would get to Warm Springs without an automobile.

Lizzie was relieved when she heard the buggy turn into the farm followed by the sound of a motor vehicle. Caleb pulled the car into the barn and hurried into the house along with his uncle.

"Mr. Jeffries agreed?" Lizzie asked.

"He drove a hard bargain, but we came to a figure that pleased him and was not too much above what I had hoped to offer. He is a shrewd business man."

"And has been his whole life," Zach said. "It is rumored he has more money than anyone would ever need, yet he does not have children or extended family."

Martha nodded in agreement. "He is like the man in Scripture who counts his profits and then dies before he can build a larger barn to hold his money."

"Yet he seems like a nice enough man," Caleb said.

"We have asked him to come for Sunday visits and dinner. He insists on staying home alone.

Your uncle checks on him at times, but he always has an excuse."

"He has too much pride," Uncle Zach said with a nod of his head. "But you have your car."

"Eat something," Martha said. "And then you can leave for town, although as I have mentioned, I do not like any of this."

"Something has to be done, Martha, so they can find their friend." Uncle Zach patted her hand. "How is your arthritis today?"

"Better because of Lizzie's help. She brought in the dried laundry and folded the linens and ironed the clothes for me."

Lizzie tried to make light of the work. "You do your own laundry always, Aunt Martha. I am glad to help when I am here."

"You are appreciated, my child."

Lizzie smiled. She liked the sound of being called *child*. Her parents never used endearing terms when they talked to her, but each person was different and she would no longer think anything but thankful thoughts about her family in Willkommen.

"Did anyone check the mail today?" she asked.

"I did," Uncle Zach said. "There was nothing in the box."

"If you get a letter," Martha said. "I will hold it for you.

"A letter?" Caleb asked.

Lizzie nodded. "I wrote my family."

He did not say anything, but she wondered what he thought. If only her parents would accept her apology and reach out to her again.

Whether that would happen, she did not know.

Eating with Uncle Zach and Aunt Martha was difficult. Lizzie was overcome with sadness. She did not want to leave and she did not want to have to dress *Englisch*. She was confused about where Caleb stood on being Amish, and she did not want to ask him. She wanted nothing else negative to cause her more worry and concern.

After the midday meal, they changed into street clothes. Lizzie wore a sweater, jeans and a jacket, and Caleb donned a similar outfit. When she stepped into the kitchen, he inhaled deeply.

"You look lovely, Lizzie. The *Englisch* clothing fits you well."

"I am more comfortable in my dress and apron." She touched her head. "I feel that something is not right without my *kapp*."

"When you came to my house that first night, you were not dressed Amish and you did not seem so concerned."

Lizzie looked around the simple kitchen where she and Aunt Martha had baked and cooked and peeled apples and made pies and kneaded bread. Over the last few days, she had stepped back into her faith. Perhaps it was his sweet aunt and uncle, but she loved being in this farmhouse and living the *plain* life.

Caleb was smiling as if finding fault with all that she was thinking.

"You are suited for the *Englisch* world?" she asked.

He shook his head. "I do not know. Time will tell."

Aunt Martha and Uncle Zach entered the kitchen, their faces tight with concern. "We will pray for *Gott*'s protection over both of you. You are doing something *gut* for another person. We will trust you will return to us unharmed."

Tears burned Lizzie's eyes from the kind and sincere words, but she blinked them back. Tears would not help today. She and Caleb needed to keep their focus on meeting the reporters and finding Emma. They had a big job ahead of them.

And if they did not succeed?

Lizzie could not think about that. They had to find Emma. They could not fail because if they failed, Emma could die.

Caleb had gone to town with his uncle a few times so he knew the way to Warm Springs. He kept the car at the speed limit and his focus on the road around them and on any vehicles that might belong to Estate Security or law enforcement. Years earlier, the town lay in ruin until four women visiting nearby Callaway Gardens detoured along the main thoroughfare and recognized the potential to turn the historical sight with its ties to Roosevelt, the polio epidemic and the Little White House into a charming venue for anyone interested in the Roosevelt era.

Their vision and hard work resurrected the dying town into a viable tourist destination. The old shops on the main street were refurbished and opened with a number of metro-Atlanta vendors setting up businesses in the original stores. The planning committee came up with innovative ideas to attract visitors, and holiday events in the remodeled town drew crowds from around the state.

"It's so quaint," Lizzie said as they drove along the main street. Raised sidewalks and porch overhangs with benches and potted plants and Christmas decorations were everywhere. Wreaths made of pine and holly adorned with festive bows hung from light posts, and twinkling white lights crossed over the street and rimmed the picture windows of the shops. Christmas trees sporting shiny gold, red and green bulbs and bedecked with multicolored lights sat in large ceramic pots. Christmas carols played over the public-address system and added to the mix that turned the small downtown area into a holiday wonderland.

"Keep watch on the various people milling along the street," Caleb instructed. "Thad Thompson and his security guard could be anywhere."

"Hopefully we'll recognize them."

"Just as long as they don't recognize you."

Lizzie nodded.

"The hotel is at the end of the block," Caleb continued. "We'll park in the rear. Be alert for anyone who seems a bit too interested in our whereabouts."

"You're worrying me, Caleb."

"I'm being cautions, which is what we both need to be. Cautious and careful."

"I hope Jeb is at the hotel."

"If not, we'll have to find a pay phone and try to contact him."

Lizzie chuckled. "Pay phones are nonexistent these days."

"Perhaps, but you never know what you'll find in a small town like this."

"Where's the rehab center?" she asked.

"Not far from here."

They parked behind the hotel. "Stay next to me, Lizzie, and keep your head down and don't make eye contact with anyone."

"You make me feel like a pariah."

"I don't want anyone to zero in on you. Act nonchalant."

"That's hard to do when I'm so worried."

"I understand."

An ice-cream shop sat at the side of the hotel. Caleb motioned her forward. "We can enter the hotel lobby through the ice-cream shop."

The clerk behind the counter smiled. "Welcome, folks."

Caleb nodded in greeting and hurried through the doors that led into the hotel. The parlor was decorated in period pieces and made him feel like he had stepped back in time.

A large hotel desk stretched across the opposite side of the room. The door to the street on the right was flanked with tall windows that looked out onto Broad Street. Christmas carols played in the background.

A wooden phone booth sat next to the front desk. A plaque recounted how newspaper reporters used that very phone booth to notify their home offices about President Roosevelt's passing.

Caleb could imagine the frenzy as the reporters elbowed each other to get to the phone and file their stories.

It was from Warm Springs that a train took Roosevelt's body and began the ride through the countryside to Washington, DC. People lined the tracks to pay their respects to the president they'd loved.

A clerk hurried from a back room. "May I help you folks?"

"We're here to see Jeb Grayson. Could you tell us which room is his?"

"I'll call Mr. Grayson and notify him that you're here to see him. What's your name, sir?"

"Tell him a friend from the coffee shop."

The clerk frowned but placed the call and relayed the message.

"He'll be down in a minute," he said after disconnecting.

Lizzie sat in a chair in the corner where she could see the street, as well as the stairway leading down from the second floor. Caleb joined her there.

The sound of footsteps caused them to glance up as Jeb hurried downstairs. He thanked the clerk, and then shook hands with Caleb and nodded to Lizzie.

"We can talk in my room. The AJC reporter I told you about will join us shortly."

They followed him upstairs. A large central room at the top of the stairs served as a dining area filled with a number of long tables and side chairs. Finely crafted antique buffets and sideboards lined the walls. A Tiffany lamp, large candelabra and a number of porcelain tureens and a silver coffee-and-tea service were situated around the room. Vases with colorful bouquets of flowers adorned the tables.

"Breakfast is served in this central dining area," Jeb explained. He led them to a guest room off the dining area, keyed open the door and motioned them inside. The room was spacious with two double beds, an antique rolltop desk, a side chest and a bureau with a mirror. Glass lamps sat on the bedside tables.

"As you've probably noted," Jeb said, "the hotel is filled with antiques. The furniture in this room was popular in the 1930s and '40s and was made by the Val-Kill Shop that Eleanor Roosevelt started in order to provide jobs for the unemployed."

He pointed to the window above the door. "In the days before air-conditioning, opening the interior window helped circulate air and provide a cross breeze. The pull bell by the door summoned help from the front desk."

"The hotel appears to have been top of the line in its day," Caleb said.

Jeb nodded. "Today it's a true step-back-in-time type of place, a real jewel that draws history lovers who want to immerse themselves in the Roosevelt period."

Lizzie took in the antiques and then glanced out the front window that looked onto the main street. "The town is charming."

Jeb moved the desk chair closer to the two side seats and motioned for Caleb and Lizzie to sit. "We'll keep our voices low. Sound travels in this old place, but we're safer here than in the lobby."

"What have you found out?" Caleb sat next to Lizzie. Jeb settled into the desk chair.

"Mr. Thompson should have arrived this morning. His security team is scouting out the area, from what a source said, to ensure no one plans to do Mr. Thompson harm."

"You mean they're searching for Lizzie?"

"I would imagine she's on their list. I'm keeping a low profile too."

"Where's Thompson staying?"

"Most of the people attending the symposium are staying at Callaway Gardens. It's about sixteen miles away. A lovely resort area. I doubt the Hotel Warm Springs would be good enough for Mr. Thompson. Nor would the outlying small local hotels suit his needs."

"What's going on today?"

"There's a parade that will start the town's weekend festivities and draw a fairly sizeable crowd. The symposium kicked off this morning. There's a cocktail party tonight. Everything ends after lunch tomorrow."

A tap sounded at the door. Jeb looked through the peephole before opening the door. A man, five-ten with gray hair pulled into a ponytail at the nap of his neck, entered the room.

He nodded to Caleb and extended his hand. "Harold Fraser."

Caleb accepted the handshake. "You're with the AJC?"

"That's right." The reporter shook Lizzie's hand. "Jeb told me about your situation. I thought you were Amish."

"I am," Lizzie said. "We dressed *Englisch* today so we wouldn't stand out in the crowd."

"Good idea."

He pointed to Jeb. "Has he been filling you in?"

Caleb nodded. "To the fact that Thompson's security team has been in town and he arrived this morning."

"That's what we've been able to uncover. I checked out the hotel in Callaway Gardens. Signs are up welcoming the symposium attendees. The program lasts the entire day. The town hosts a parade. Lots of floats and fun events for children. The symposium runs through Saturday morning followed by a lunch for some of the special-needs children and adults in the area. A few of the folks from the symposium will be there. Roosevelt hosted dinners for the polio patients. The rehab center is following that tradition. The winner of the Southeast Humanitarian Award will be the guest of honor."

"Does Thompson have a chance of winning?"

The reporter nodded. "That's the rumor."

"What's he doing after the symposium?" Caleb asked.

"He'll fly back to Sarasota in the afternoon."

"There's a party tomorrow night," Lizzie volunteered. "He's hosting a small gathering of campaign supporters at his estate."

She looked at Caleb. "To announce his run for the senate. Which means Andrew will have his sights on Emma if she's at the rehab center and grab her once his father is out of town. Our deadline to save Emma is Saturday afternoon before Mr. Thompson leaves town."

"What makes you think she's at the rehab center?" Jeb asked.

Caleb explained about her disappearance from Respite Haven and what Ruben had shared.

"Thompson isn't to be trusted," Harold said. "Everything points to him scamming Medicaid, but so far, I can't prove anything."

"From what we've learned, Emma seems to have been given medication that wasn't prescribed to keep her quiet. Is that the proof you are looking for?" Lizzie asked.

"That's exactly the type of information I need. If someone checks the books, I'm sure they'll find all kinds of irregularities, but there has to be a reason to go searching in the first place. If you find that friend of yours, see if she would give her statement to the authorities."

"I'm not sure she would be willing to come forward. I have a feeling she's been brainwashed into thinking she's being protected instead of being held against her will. We had planned to visit the rehab center in hopes we would find her there, although if Mr. Thompson is at the same facility, we might need to change our plans and go later in the afternoon when the symposium is over for the day and he's back at his hotel."

"Whatever happens," the AJC reporter said, "convince your friend to talk to us."

"First we have to find her."

"I could call the rehab center," Harold offered, "and ask to speak to her."

"You might alert their suspicions, which would cause more harm than good. Plus, she's probably registered under an alias."

"That would be Warren Whitaker's doing and not the rehab center." Harold held up his hand. "I should have mentioned this earlier. The Warm Springs rehab center is a legitimate healthcare facility that has never had a problem. I don't mean to imply that they're involved with Thompson or his brother-in-law. Your friend may be there for an evaluation, but I doubt she would be held against her will or for anything other than actual rehab needs."

"And if she's not at the rehab center, then where is Emma being held?" Lizzie asked.

"Your guess is as good as mine," the reporter said with a shrug.

Harold's response did not help Lizzie. She needed to find Emma and she needed to find her before Saturday afternoon.

TWENTY-FOUR

Leaving the hotel was complicated by the parade. Caleb and Lizzie stood outside the ice-cream parlor, somewhat protected from view by the side of the building, and watched the various floats pass by on the street. More activities would take place over the weekend, but Friday was a crowd-drawing day and many retired folks flocked to the quaint historic area for the official start of the festivities.

"As you mentioned upstairs, visiting the rehab center today might be too risky," he told Lizzie.

"Let's see how things seem after the parade. The crowds might thin out by then."

Caleb was uneasy as he studied the tourists going from store to store. A number of men sat on the benches as if waiting for their wives to finish shopping. A deputy sheriff's car slowly moved along Broad Street. Caleb ushered Lizzie back into the sweet shop until the cruiser had passed.

He wanted to get Lizzie out of the crowd before the parade started. The sound of a band playing told him he had waited too long.

The exit from the rear parking area was blocked by local volunteers wearing fluorescent vests. One of the men instructed the pedestrians to clear the street and move onto the raised sidewalks.

Lizzie stepped closer to Caleb. "I haven't been to a parade in a long time."

"This isn't what I wanted to do today. Especially when we need to find Emma. Did you see the deputy's car?"

"Was it the same officer who stopped at your aunt and uncle's house?"

"I couldn't tell. Stay back in case he returns."

The band from a local high school passed by followed by an ROTC honor guard that carried the American flag and the flag of Georgia. The people cheered and waved tiny US flags in the air.

"Everyone loves a parade," Caleb muttered.

A number of vintage cars drove slowly along the road. Young girls wearing rhinestone tiaras waved to the onlookers.

"There's Miss Warm Springs," Lizzie said, as a convertible passed with a pretty girl perched on the back seat.

A church float rolled by with people dressed in period costumes singing a medley of Christmas songs and waving to the crowd.

Horns honked and people cheered.

The next float was a flatbed truck. People sat on bales of hay and threw candy to the crowd. Some of the adults had visible disabilities. A slender woman stood at the rear of the truck bed and stared vapidly into space while others waved and tossed candy.

Lizzie tugged on Caleb's arm. "Look at that float."

"You want some candy?" he teased.

"Check out the woman in the green dress and black coat."

The truck had already passed in front of them. Caleb stepped closer to the road and stared after the float, hoping to catch sight of the woman in green. At that moment, a big burly man wearing a cowboy hat sidled in front of Caleb, blocking his view.

Lizzie pointed to the float. "Did you see her?"

He shook his head. "Someone got in my way. Who was it?"

"Didn't you see her, Caleb? It was Emma!"

"We need to follow the float." Lizzie hurried along the sidewalk. Her concern that Andrew might still be in town was overridden by her desire to find Emma. Tourists lined the street, and she had difficulty making her way through the throng of people.

"Excuse me," she said, feeling overwhelmed by the dense crowd. She glanced back to ensure Caleb was behind her. They needed to reach the end of the parade route by the time the truck stopped so they could meet up with Emma.

Lizzie's pulse raced, and she grew more frustrated when the people refused to move. The next three floats threw candy, which increased the ruckus. With everyone—children and adults—scrambling for candy, their path was blocked even more.

"We have to hurry," she told Caleb, but there was no way to shove through the throng any faster than they already were.

At the end of the street, the parade vehicles turned left into a parking area.

"There." She pointed ahead. "I can see the flat-bed."

They continued to weave through the crowd. As they neared the truck, her heart sank. The flatbed was empty.

"Oh, Caleb, she's gone."

A man stood near the open driver's door.

"Sir?" Caleb called to him. "Can you tell us where the people on that float were from?"

"The adult home for people with disabilities out on Lucas Road."

"Lucas Road?"

"North of town. Follow this street about three miles and turn left at the four-way stop. Go about two more miles and you'll see the turnoff on your right."

"Is there a sign?" Caleb asked.

The guy shook his head. "No sign, but it's the first roadway after the stop sign. You'll find it easy enough."

"What about the people who were riding in the truck. Are they still in town?" Lizzie asked.

"They went back to the home."

"Do you know anyone there?"

"Only Warren Whitaker. He's the one who contacted me about using my truck."

"The manager of Respite Haven?"

"I'm not sure. All I know is that he wanted the folks to ride in the parade."

"Thank you." Lizzie turned back to Caleb. "You got the directions? We have to go there now before something happens to Emma."

"You're sure it was her?"

"I'm positive. She was thinner and her hair was different, but it has to be Emma."

"The parade will be over by the time we get to the car. We can take the road west of town so we don't run into the police or any of the county deputy sheriffs."

"Speaking of police," she said, her gaze on the cop car parked farther down the street.

The officer was standing by his vehicle. He stared at Lizzie, then spoke into his shoulder radio.

Her stomach tightened.

"Come on," Caleb prompted. "We need to get out of here."

The cop started to weave through the mass of people and headed toward them.

Caleb grabbed her hand and pulled her through the crowd. The street pulsed with activity as the people flocked to the end of the parade staging area.

"Let's cross the street. There's a courtyard filled with shops that might offer more cover."

Lizzie glanced back. "Hurry, Caleb. The officer is coming this way."

They crossed the street, entered one of the stores and exited through a back door that led to the large outdoor courtyard lined with gift shops.

Caleb motioned her forward. "Let's go behind that next building."

They hurried along a narrow path, then stepped into an antique store and, once again, left through a rear exit.

Lizzie peered around the side of the building. The cop had entered the courtyard and was staring at the crowd. A second cop joined him.

"There are two of them now," she said.

"The coffee shop." Caleb pointed to the small eatery.

They stepped inside. He ordered two coffees, then grabbed newspapers off one of the tables. He handed a section to Lizzie, and they both settled into chairs and held up the newspapers to cover their faces as if they were reading.

Hearing the door open, Lizzie peered around the edge of the paper just as one of the police officers stepped inside and waved a greeting to the guy behind the counter.

"How 'bout a cup of Joe," the barista offered.

"No thanks, Kurt, but I'll take a rain check."

"Everything okay, Doug?"

"I'm looking for a couple of outsiders."

The guy behind the counter chuckled. "Everyone's an outsider if he doesn't live in Warm Springs."

The cop laughed. "You've got a point. On second thought, I'll take that cup of coffee. My partner could use a pick me up too."

"Two coffees on the house," the clerk said.

Lizzie's hands trembled, and she was sure the paper she was holding was shaking. The cop and the clerk continued to chat until the to-go cups of coffee were poured.

"Thanks." The cop headed for the door. "Have a good day."

Lizzie sighed with relief when the door slammed and the officer handed his buddy one of the cups. They eyed the crowd for a long moment and then left the central courtyard.

"Let's go." Caleb folded the paper and waved goodbye to the clerk.

Once outside, he pointed her in the opposite direction than the officers had gone. "We need to cross the street to get to the car. Or you can wait here and I'll pick you up at the corner."

"No way. I'm staying with you."

The crowd had thinned, which meant they would be even more visible. On the far side of the street, they spied the two policemen sipping coffee.

A group of schoolchildren wearing matching

T-shirts approached them along with their chaperones.

"Blend in with the kids," Caleb suggested.

"What?"

"We'll look like school chaperones if we cross the street with the children. Act like you fit in."

With her pounding heart and trembling hands, Lizzie felt more like a Christmas grinch than a chaperon, but following Caleb's prompting, she stepped into the crowd of children and started across the street.

Sensing something was wrong, she glanced back. Caleb had stopped walking and was staring at a car angled into a parking space on the opposite side of the road. A sports car convertible.

Her heart pounded. Andrew's car.

She hurried across the street, climbed the steps to the raised walkway and stopped in her tracks as a man stepped from one of the stores. Tall and muscular with a bandage on his neck.

Fear coursed through her veins.

Andrew's face twisted in rage.

Run! her inner voice prompted.

She dashed around the children, raced along the porch and stumbled down the steps. Her heartbeat sounded in her ears. She turned into the alley and ran to the rear of the next building.

Footsteps pounded the pavement. Andrew was following close behind her.

Caleb's car sat parked behind the hotel. She

needed to hide, but the vehicle would offer no protection.

Where could she go?

Glancing left, she spied the ice-cream shop and hurried inside. No one was at the counter. She passed through the side door that led into the hotel. The lobby was empty. She pulled in a lungful of air, then charged up the stairs, ran across the dining area and stopped short at Jeb Grayson's room.

She tapped lightly on the door. "Please," she cried silently. "Please, open the door."

Her pulse raced, her hands trembled and she gasped, hearing Andrew in the lobby below call her name.

Heavy footsteps pounded up the stairs.

She glanced around the dining area. None of the antiques provided a place to hide. Again, she tapped on the door.

"Elizabeth!" Andrew called her name. At any moment, he would race up the final flight of stairs and see her trembling in the far corner of the dining area.

"Please," she moaned under her breath.

The door to the guest room opened. Jeb's eyes widened.

She pushed past him, closed the door behind her and held a finger to her lips.

Glancing up, she saw the breezeway window

above the door was cocked open. Any noise they made would carry into the central dining room.

Footsteps sounded outside the door. "Elizabeth?"

Fearful of being found, she shook her head, willing Jeb to remain silent. Neither of them moved. The rapid beat of Lizzie's heart continued to echo in her ears.

What was happening on the other side of the guest-room door? She imagined Andrew with his head tilted, waiting for the slightest sound that would reveal her whereabouts.

Seconds ticked by ever so slowly, until at last he exhaled a deep, guttural sigh. The sound floated through the transom window followed by footsteps racing down the stairs. She let out the breath she was holding and almost collapsed onto the floor.

Jeb hurried to the window and peered around the curtain. "A tall guy with dark hair just ran from the hotel. He's heading toward a convertible sports car parked on the street."

She stepped closer and watched Andrew climb behind the wheel. He backed the sports car onto the street, drove past the hotel and disappeared out of sight.

Another knock sounded at the door. Her heart nearly stopped again.

"Jeb, it's Caleb. Is Lizzie with you?"

Relief swept over her. She crossed the room

and opened the door ever so slowly. Seeing Caleb, she let out a gasp of relief and fell into his arms.

Caleb wrapped her tightly in his embrace and stroked her hair. "I thought Andrew had found you." His voice was thick with emotion.

She soaked in his strength for a long moment, grateful they were together again. Then realizing they weren't alone, she pulled back and pointed to the newsman still standing by the window.

"Thanks to Jeb, I survived. Andrew just drove off. I'm worried that he's searching for Emma. We have to find her before Andrew gets to her."

"Remember, nothing is going to happen until after the symposium," Caleb assured her.

"You're right, but I don't trust Andrew. The sooner we find Emma, the better."

After thanking Jeb again, they explained about seeing the woman on the float and being chased by the officers and Andrew. They then hurried back to their car.

"Keep your head down," Caleb suggested once they buckled their seat belts.

"This is becoming a habit," she admitted.

"Anything to keep you safe, Lizzie."

Which she appreciated. "Do you see the cops anywhere?"

"Not at the moment. We'll drive west, then turn north on a parallel road. When we're about a mile out of town, we'll head back to the main road and then stay on it until we find the four-way stop."

"We have to find Emma."

"As long as the woman in the float was Emma."

Caleb was right. Lizzie had seen a woman who looked something like her old friend, but in hindsight, she had reservations. As much as she wanted to find Emma, she could have imagined the similarity. *Oh* Gott, *let me find her before it is too late.*

TWENTY-FIVE

Caleb was more than worried. He feared everything was about to blow up in their faces. Lizzie thought the woman on the float was Emma.

Or was she someone else who looked like Emma?

He wasn't sure.

Neither was Lizzie. She remained slumped down in the seat.

"We're outside of town," Caleb said. "No cars in sight if you want to sit up."

"Are we on the right road?"

"As far as I can tell we are." He looked at the odometer. "We've gone about three miles. The four-way stop should come up fairly soon."

Lizzie sat upright and stared out the passenger window. "There's not much out here except woods."

"I hope the truck driver knew what he was talking about with the directions." He also hoped the guy hadn't directed them into a trap.

"Suppose it wasn't Emma," Lizzie said, her voice low and riddled with angst.

"Let's deal with that problem when we come to it. Right now, we're following the only lead we have. An adult home for people with disabilities would be the perfect place for Whitaker to house

Emma, especially if he has something to do with overseeing the facility."

"Which means Mr. Thompson would know where to find her and Andrew would, as well."

The four-way stop appeared. "So far the directions have been correct."

Lizzie watched the road ahead as they passed through the intersection. "There's the turnoff."

The drive angled back through the wooded area. They came to a clearing and a long ranch-style home appeared ahead. A small sign read Country Manor.

"How do you want to handle this?" he asked.

"I guess we should knock on the door and see if we can talk to her."

Caleb parked, rounded the car and opened Lizzie's door. "Let's not give too much away."

She nodded. They hurried to the home and rang the bell. When no one answered, they knocked and then tried the bell again.

A bulky man with collar length hair and a tattoo on his thick neck answered the door. "Yah?"

Lizzie smiled. "I have a friend who lives here and wondered if I could see her. She was a resident at Respite Haven and moved to Country Manor a few months ago."

"You mean Gloria?"

"May I see her?"

"I'll have to get permission."

"We're old friends. I was driving by and wanted to say hello."

"You still need to get cleared. Plus, Gloria's resting now."

"Wasn't she in town for the parade?"

"That's right."

"Then she hasn't been home long. Are you sure she can't be disturbed?"

"Look, ma'am. Gloria needs her rest. The trip to Warm Springs can be overwhelming for our residents. You'll have to come back tomorrow. If you want to leave your name, I'll tell her you stopped by."

"Just let her know an old friend from the North Georgia mountains wanted to say hello. What time should I come back tomorrow?"

"Later in the afternoon. About four p.m."

Walking to the car, Lizzie sidled close to Caleb. "Let's park in the woods and circle back," she whispered. "I want to watch what happens next."

He did as she asked and pulled the car off the path, closer to the main road. They both hiked back through the woods and watched the house. Nothing changed.

Lizzie pointed to the rear of the building. "It looks like there might be a back porch."

They traipsed farther into the woods, careful not to make any noise. Lizzie pointed to the screened-in porch where two male residents sat in plastic lawn chairs. She sighed with discouragement. "I don't think we'll see Emma today."

"Wait." Caleb grabbed her arm and nodded toward the porch.

A tall woman in a green dress and a black jacket stepped into the screened enclosure. The men nodded a greeting and then went inside.

"That's the woman I saw on the float. Stay here, Caleb, and wave to me if you see the caregiver."

"Be careful, Lizzie."

He had been worried ever since leaving town, and he was even more worried now as Lizzie walked quickly across the clearing. She was visible to anyone from Country Manor who looked out the windows. The caregiver was a big guy with a tough-as-nails attitude, who wouldn't appreciate Lizzie going against the rules. No telling what he would do if he saw her.

Lizzie hurried toward the porch, her heart pounding. She feared she might be seen and was equally anxious about finding Emma. Knowing Andrew was in the area only compounded her concern.

The way the woman stood with her weight on one foot was how Emma used to stand when she was studying something in the distance. Lizzie pulled in a breath and approached the porch.

No doubt sensing movement, the woman

turned toward Lizzie. Her eyes widened. She gasped and took a step back.

Tears of joy burned Lizzie's eyes and a flood of relief swept over her. At long last, she had found her friend.

"Don't be afraid, Emma. It's me. It's Lizzie. Remember? From Willkommen? I've been looking for you for so long. Are you okay?"

Emma glanced at the house and wrung her hands. Her brow furrowed.

"Don't be afraid." Lizzie placed her hand on the screen, wishing she could reach through the mesh and reassure Emma with a hug.

"We played together as girls. We would run through the pasture and pretend we were invincible. Caleb played with us sometimes." Lizzie paused for a moment to see if his name brought a response. "You and Caleb liked each other growing up and you told me you planned to marry."

Emma shook her head.

"It is true, Emma. Caleb is a good man. He has been worried about you. I have worried too."

Abruptly Emma turned and scurried back into the house. The porch door slammed behind her.

Unsettled by Emma's rejection, Lizzie hung her head and moaned. Hot tears stung her eyes as she backtracked to where Caleb waited. He opened his arms and pulled her close.

"She was afraid of me," Lizzie whispered, hearing the pain in her own voice.

"It is hard, *yah*? But remember, they are drugging her."

"I know." Drawing comfort from his understanding, she pulled back. "At least we've found her. Now we have to convince her to leave with us."

Caleb glanced at the house. "I wish we could notify law enforcement."

"They would side with Mr. Thompson, and I would end up in jail. You might as well, Caleb."

"If I thought it would bring about Emma's release, it would be worth being jailed, but I fear it would not end well for her."

The front door opened, and the caregiver stepped outside. He held a cell phone to his ear.

"Can you hear what he's saying?" she whispered.

"Something about she's here, and I'll see you Saturday."

"He's talking about Emma."

"We don't know that for sure."

A squirrel skittered up a nearby tree and dropped a nut. The sound echoed.

The caregiver looked in their direction.

Caleb pulled Lizzie back, deeper into the woods. "It's time to go."

She hesitated. "I don't want to leave Emma."

The squirrel jumped to a nearby tree.

The caregiver pocketed his phone and stared in their direction.

"Come on." Caleb grabbed her arm.

Lizzie looked back, then turned to hurry after Caleb. A root snagged her foot and she tripped. Caleb caught her just before she crashed to the ground.

"Are you okay?" he asked.

She nodded. "Thanks."

"Hey," the caregiver yelled. "Who's there?"

Caleb put his arm around Lizzie's waist and hurried her around the underbrush.

"What are you doing?" the caregiver's voice sounded.

They ran to the car and climbed in. Caleb started the engine and accelerated. The car jostled over the bumpy road.

Lizzie looked back. "The caregiver has returned the phone to his ear. I hope he's not calling for help."

Law enforcement or Estate Security? Both groups were looking for her.

The main road appeared ahead. The shrill squeal of a siren sounded in the distance. Lizzie's heart pounded and her mouth went dry.

"Don't let them find us, Caleb."

"Hold on."

He turned right onto the main road, heading away from town.

"This old car isn't made for high speeds. Let's hope we get out of this area before the cops arrive."

Lizzie closed her eyes. "*Gott*, help us," she moaned, her hands joined together in prayer.

The siren drew closer, then stopped.

"I'm guessing they turned on the dirt road that leads to the home," Caleb said.

"Which gives us more time." But would it give them enough time to get to safety?

TWENTY-SIX

Night was falling by the time Caleb and Lizzie neared Ruben's farm. "We need to tell him we found Emma."

"AKA Susanna." Lizzie glanced back, checking the road. "Going back to your aunt and uncle's house would be a mistake since the deputy sheriff stopped there this morning."

"Ruben might be able to put us up for the night."

Caleb turned into the Amish man's drive and parked near the barn. Lizzie rolled down the window and waved as Ruben stepped onto the porch. "You do not recognize us without the buggy."

"I am surprised. You bought an automobile?"

"Caleb's renting it from his uncle's neighbor. Would you mind if we park in your barn? We don't want anyone to know we're here."

He hurried to open both barn doors and stood to the side as Caleb drove into the barn and cut the engine.

Climbing out of the car, he shook Ruben's hand and patted his back. "We have news."

"About Susanna?"

Lizzie nodded. "We found our friend Emma. If she is the same person as you know from Respite Haven, then Susanna has been found, as well."

"I am eager to learn where she is." He pointed

to the house. "But first, let us go inside. I was cooking dinner. You can stay?"

"Perhaps longer than you expected," Caleb said with a smile. "Dinner sounds *wunderbaar*, if you have plenty."

"I have cooked more than I need, but you have made me eager to hear your news."

They entered the house, wiped their feet on the small rug by the door and hung their coats on the wall pegs.

"Come to the woodstove." Ruben motioned them forward. "The night has turned cold."

Lizzie held her hands up, appreciating the warmth. "Once the sun goes down, the temperature drops, but you are anxious to hear about Emma." She explained about the parade and seeing her on the float.

"You are sure it was Emma?"

"Caleb did not get as good of a view of her, but I was convinced it was Emma. We hurried to the end of the parade route, hoping to find her there."

Ruben's initial enthusiasm faltered. "You lost sight of her?"

Lizzie recounted their conversation with the truck driver. "She's staying at a home for adults with development disabilities. It is called Country Manor. Have you ever been there?"

Ruben shook his head.

"The director of the home is the same man who runs Respite Haven."

"Warren Whitaker?" Ruben asked.

Lizzie nodded. "Thad Thompson's brother-in-law."

"Now I understand. He moved Susanna to the other facility to have better control over her. We have to save her."

"You are right, Ruben, although I do not know how to get her out of the house." She told him about being chased by Andrew Thompson and her fear that he planned to do Emma harm. "We need to save Emma before Andrew grabs her."

"I have an idea that might work," Ruben volunteered. "It involves a call I got earlier today from the Warm Springs rehab center."

"Were you offered a job?"

"Of sorts. It is something that will put my voice to good use."

Caleb looked at Lizzie. They both shrugged. "Tell us."

"There is a lunch at the rehab center tomorrow. President Roosevelt hosted meals there for the children at the polio center. The organizers of the symposium thought it would be a fitting way to conclude their event since recognition will be given to a few noted people who have made a difference in rehabilitation."

"One of the newspaper reporters we know mentioned the event. So how do you fit in?"

"The guests invited to the lunch are the special-needs children in the area and those at the rehab center. There is another facility that will be included. It's on the text they sent me. Let me check to ensure I have the right name."

He looked at his phone and nodded. "That is what I thought. The other facility represented will be the home for adults, Country Manor."

"And you will be there to help?"

"I'll be there to perform with a few Amish singers. We are joining a group of Old English carolers dressed in period costumes. Following the luncheon, the Amish singers will leave in my wagon and drive through town, waving to the crowd. There will be an area set aside where we will perform again."

Lizzie smiled. "What about the Old English carolers?"

He nodded. "They will follow in a second wagon. After our performance at the rehab center, we will chat with the children and adults and hand out presents. When the event concludes, I'll drive the wagon through town and stop on Broad Street for the final performance."

"By the hotel?" Caleb asked.

"Near there and then more toys will be given out. Many of the merchants have hosted toy drives and visitors over the last few months have been generous. It will be a special day for the children in the area."

"And a perfect time with all the commotion to grab Emma."

"I will need help at the luncheon," Ruben said.

"They will not allow us to attend," Lizzie said, her smile waning.

"The lady in the personnel department said more English carolers were needed."

"Carolers?"

Ruben nodded. "There are enough Amish singers, but they still need a few more dressed in costume. I have material. We can make outfits for you tonight."

"Victorian Dickens Christmas carolers? Old English costumes?" Lizzie asked.

He nodded. "I have my wife's sewing machine."

"You want me to be a caroler?" Caleb raised his brow in disbelief.

Ruben laughed. "You will be great."

"With the three of us there—" Lizzie glanced at Caleb "—we should be able to talk to Emma and hopefully get her away from the caregiver."

"It seems to be our only option," Caleb admitted. "If you can make the costumes, Lizzie, I can pretend to be a caroler."

"It's got to work." Lizzie reached for the fabric in the box Ruben set on the floor near the table.

Masquerading as carolers would be risky, but it was the only way they could get to Emma.

Lizzie started working on the costumes as soon as they finished dinner. Caleb helped Ruben with the dishes and then sat in the rocker and refreshed her coffee cup as needed.

"What time are you leaving in the morning to get to the luncheon?" she asked Ruben.

"By ten o'clock."

She glanced at the wall clock in the kitchen. "That gives me more than enough time. I'll make a long skirt for myself. If only I had my cape and black bonnet."

"You can use my wife's."

"You would not mind?"

"It would be put to good use."

"I'll add lace to the bonnet and create a muff."

"What about for me?" Caleb asked.

Ruben went upstairs and came back with a black waistcoat. "Perhaps you can embellish this old worn coat that I had planned to discard. If you add lace at the neck and do something with my old black hat, Caleb will look like he hails from England of old."

She nodded. "I'll turn it into a top hat by cutting the brim and expanding the sides. It just might work."

Ruben pulled out a box of his wife's clothing. "Use whatever you need. If you do not mind, I will retire for the night. There is a guest room at the top of the stairs when you get tired and another one off the kitchen."

"Thank you," Lizzie said as she started to work on the waistcoat for Caleb.

He rolled his eyes and chuckled when she added lace to the front of the jacket. "This is not the type of outfit I usually wear."

"But you'll look like a character in a Dickens novel." She smiled.

"Just so we fit in with the rest of the carolers."

"We'll keep a low profile. Ruben said the symposium award winner will attend the luncheon, as well." She glanced at Caleb. "Do you know what I'm thinking?"

He nodded. "That if Thad Thompson wins, he'll be at the luncheon. No telling what he will do if he spots you, Lizzie."

"We'll be on the lookout for him."

Caleb spied the cell phone Ruben had placed on the kitchen table. "I'll call Jeb, and let him know our plans."

"See if he has learned anything more about Thompson and his son and brother-in-law," she added.

Caleb made the call, hit the Speaker button and stepped closer to where Lizzie was working.

"Thad Thompson attended the cocktail party at Callaway Gardens," Jeb quickly informed them. "He's returned to his hotel. Neither Harold nor I have seen Andrew, but Estate Security has a number of cars on the premises. The guards are staying at the same hotel as their boss."

"They're ensuring he remains safe," Caleb said with a nod. "And providing an alibi if anything happens that points to Thompson's involvement should Emma go missing."

Lizzie held up her hand. "Do not mention anything like that. I am already concerned enough about her well-being."

"We have to be practical," Caleb continued. "Mr. Thompson and Andrew are in town. They're both eager to get rid of Emma and that means we must act fast."

Caleb told Jeb about their plans for the next day.

"Stay safe," the reporter said before he disconnected.

"Suppose Emma doesn't go to the luncheon?" Lizzie raised her brow as she guided the fabric through the sewing machine. "We're doing all this convinced that they'll allow her to attend. Plans could change."

"If we don't see her, we'll race to Country Manor and find a way to get inside."

"You make it sound so easy."

"I know that won't be the case, but we need to remain optimistic and think of all our options."

"I wish we had more time." Lizzie held up Caleb's outfit. "Your costume is done. I just need to finish mine."

"Is there nothing you cannot do?"

She laughed, enjoying his kind words. "And you are full of flattery. What would your father say?"

"That I am speaking the truth and that he too can see how industrious you are and how you are determined to find Emma."

"Did your father approve of Emma?"

"Approve?"

"As a future daughter-in-law?"

He shook his head. "My father and I did not talk of such things."

"I'm sure your mother did."

"My mother thought Emma was flighty and self-absorbed. She had her eye on another woman for her youngest son."

"Another woman? Do I know her?"

He leaned closer and smiled.

Her chest tightened, and for a long moment she stared into his dark eyes, admiring the depth of concern she saw there.

"My mother always thought you were delightful, Lizzie."

She blushed. "Your mother is delightful herself."

"She knew the other woman would be everything I've ever wanted."

Caleb's words confused her and the gleam in his eye threw her off-kilter. As much as she wanted to believe he was talking about her, she knew Emma was the woman who had captured Caleb's heart.

He drew even closer.

"You're talking about Emma?" she whispered.

He pulled back, seemingly frustrated by her comment. "You do not understand."

Caleb was right. She did not understand.

"I will check outside to make certain no one is hovering around the barn and outbuildings."

He left the house as she stared after him, not sure of what had just happened.

She did not understand Caleb today. What did he mean that there was another woman? Perhaps it was his fatigue that made him say such a thing. For half a heartbeat, she had thought he would kiss her again. The first time had been a mistake. Why would she think he would kiss her again, no matter how much she wanted him to?

Caleb needed fresh air as much as he needed to check the farm. With law enforcement and Estate Security searching for Lizzie, he had to be cautious and overly protective.

Emma had always been her own person and pushed the boundaries of Amish propriety, which was one of the reasons his mother struggled with her. But she did not have problems with Lizzie, who made sound decisions and put the needs of others ahead of her own.

He sighed. Growing up, he had not realized the goodness that was at the core of who Lizzie was. He had accepted it as her own personality. Recently he had started to see how unique she really was.

He tapped his toe against the side of the barn as if trying to get rid of the frustration he felt.

Everything was coming to a head. Tomorrow they would try to save Emma. Caleb had to make sure Lizzie did not get hurt.

He walked around the house, barn and outbuildings and stopped every twenty yards to stare into the distance. So far, the night was quiet. He hoped it would remain so until they had Emma safely home in Willkommen.

What would Caleb do then? Would he visit his family or would he ride by his father's farm without stopping? He would make that decision when the time came. He could not make it now.

Lizzie had gone to bed by the time Caleb returned to the house. He was too keyed up to sleep so he tossed another log into the wood-burning stove and put the coffee pot on the burner to heat. A Bible sat on a small table nearby. He reached for the leather-bound book, this one in German and let the pages open as they willed.

I the Lord search the heart, I try the reins, even to give every man according to his ways, and according to the fruit of his doings.

Once the coffee was hot, he poured a cup, grabbed his knives and the wood and returned to the porch to whittle. The moon provided enough light, and peace flowed over him as he began to work the wood.

What was the fruit of his doings? He had

turned his back on his faith and on the *Ordnung* that had guided his family for generations. Did he think he was better than the others? More worldly?

The only thing he did with any success was whittle and carve, although working with his uncle made him realize how much he loved the land. At home, he had balked at mundane tasks that never seemed to end. Was it the farm or his father that caused his upset?

If the Lord searched Caleb's heart, what would He find? A confused man who straddled a line between the Amish and *Englisch* ways of life. Caleb would have to make a decision sometime soon.

Amish or *Englisch*? He did not know which one he would choose.

TWENTY-SEVEN

Caleb parked the rented car behind the Hotel Warm Springs. He and Lizzie hurried inside to talk to Jeb. The reporter met them in the lobby and ushered them upstairs.

"Estate Security knows I'm here," Jeb said after they entered his room. "But they haven't caused a problem yet. I think it's because my buddy from the AJC is here. Harold's doing an article on the symposium and will interview the winner of the Southeast Humanitarian Award. Thad Thompson is hoping to win."

"What are his chances?" Caleb asked.

"He's built more rehab centers and nursing homes than anyone else in the Southeast. Plus, he chose isolated rural locations that have long needed good care for their seniors and the infirmed."

"You said *gut* care," Lizzie repeated.

"That's it exactly. For the most part, Thompson's long-term and rehab facilities provide adequate service. However a few of them, like the one his brother-in-law runs, have significant problems. The truth will eventually be revealed. My fear is that Thompson will throw the blame on his brother-in-law and come away without taking responsibility for what has transpired."

"I can vouch for their corruptible actions," Lizzie insisted. "I hope Emma will, as well."

"She could provide firsthand evidence that significant wrongdoing has occurred."

Caleb mentioned the nurse at Respite Haven who had moved to Ohio. "If you could track her down, she might provide information."

"Yet if she was distributing meds without a doctor's prescription, I doubt she'll say anything to incriminate herself."

Lizzie nodded. "That is true."

"The AJC has a booth set up on the street today. They'll be playing Christmas carols along with a local radio station and taking donations for needy families. We'll keep our eyes open for Andrew and Estate Security."

"Call the number I used to contact you," Caleb said. "I asked Ruben to bring his phone. We'll be working together at the luncheon."

"What about law enforcement?"

"I'm worried about them since they seem to be in with Thad Thompson. If we can pull this off without police or the sheriff department's involvement so much the better."

Jeb nodded. "You folks are doing a lot of good. Probably more than you know. It's one thing to be a cheat and a liar. It's another thing to bring harm to the infirmed, those with dementia and the aged. I don't have any pity for Thompson and his organization, and the sooner the truth comes out, the better."

Caleb looked at the clock on the dresser. "It's time for us to head to the rehab center."

"I'll drive you, so you can leave your car parked here."

"That will help."

The ride did not take long. Jeb dropped them off at a side entrance where two hay wagons were parked, hitched to teams of draft horses. The wagons were decorated for Christmas, and the horses had red-and-green ribbons braided into their manes and tails.

"Be careful," Jeb warned, as they climbed from his car and hurried to where Ruben stood.

"Get into your caroler costumes," he instructed as they approached him. "The bonnet will offer some protection, Lizzie. Turn you head if you see anyone you recognize."

She and Caleb slipped their costumes over their clothing.

"Where are the other singers?" she asked.

"In one of the side rooms. They are having lunch. The program starts after the guests finish eating."

"I'm too nervous to eat," Lizzie admitted.

Caleb squeezed her hand. "This will work."

Once inside, Ruben handed them the sheet

music. "Hold this up when you're singing and stand behind me so you are less noticeable."

Lizzie explained that Jeb might try to contact them.

"I'll keep my phone on vibrate in case he calls," Ruben assured them. "Whoever spots Emma can let the others know. After we sing, we're supposed to mix and mingle with the invited guests. The children will be given small presents. The adults will receive lap blankets and boxes of candy. In the excitement of the gift giving, we will head to the wagon and leave the area. The route takes us to the eastern edge of Broad Street and then through town with a stop at the AJC booth, near the hotel."

"Is that where we transfer Emma out of the wagon and into the car?" Lizzie asked.

Caleb nodded. "That's the plan."

Ruben was big and tall—he would dwarf Lizzie when she stood behind him. Caleb would be more visible, but his photo had not been featured in the newspaper, and it was doubtful law enforcement had him in their crosshairs.

Lizzie was a different story.

"What if Emma isn't in the audience?" she asked the question that continued to trouble her.

"We talked about this before," Caleb said. "We'll leave as quickly as possible, hurry to the car and race to the home."

"And if we don't find her there?"

"Lizzie, trust that *Gott* will work all things together for *gut*."

Ruben nodded. "My mother always said that."

"So did mine, and we both should listen and adhere to what our mothers said."

Hearing Caleb quote Scripture brought Lizzie comfort, but when she glanced at the sheet music, her stomach tightened. "I'm not the best singer."

He laughed. "My brothers said my voice could scare the dairy cows into not producing milk, but we'll mouth the words and rely on the other members of the choir to carry the performance."

A man from the rehab center entered the room where the choir waited. "The folks have finished lunch," he said. "Once dessert is served, I'll call you in. The audience is enthused. I know they'll enjoy your concert."

"There are some special guests today?" one of the men asked.

"A few people from the rehab symposium. You'll open with a song, then the winner of the prestigious Southeast Humanitarian Award will be recognized. After he says a few words, I'll turn the program over to you again."

Lizzie's stomach was in knots. For the last three years, she had wondered about Emma. Seeing her yesterday had been good and bad. Good because they had found her. Bad because Emma was fearful and had turned away from Lizzie. What would happen if she did the same today?

"It's time." The man directing the program motioned them forward.

Lizzie and Caleb walked behind Ruben. A few singers followed after them. The dining room was long and narrow, and the floor was covered in alternating black-and-white tiles. A photograph hanging on the wall showed President Roosevelt enjoying a festive meal with polio patients in the very same room.

From what Lizzie had deduced, the rehab center wanted today to be both festive and historic, yet if Thad Thompson was recognized, he was anything but notable and his business dealings were corrupt. The way he covered up for his son's transgressions and secreted women away from the public eye when Andrew's attacks left them injured was criminal. Lizzie could think of nothing but the injustice that had been done to Emma.

The chatter in the dining room was jovial. Some of the children waved. Others were focused on what appeared to be the pecan pie topped with ice cream that sat on the tables before them.

Trying not to be obvious, Lizzie glanced around the room. Where was Emma?

At the head table, she saw Thad Thompson and his brother-in-law. When they glanced in her direction, she turned her head. If only she could find Emma.

"I see Susanna." Ruben nodded almost imperceptibly to a table in the rear of the room where a number of adults were seated. Two were in wheelchairs.

Lizzie followed his gaze. Her heart leaped with joy when she spied the thin woman she had approached on the porch at the group home. The woman had appeared fearful and nervous yesterday. Today, her shoulders were back and her eyes intense as she stared at Lizzie and held her gaze as if she was the old Emma, the feisty friend who lived life to the fullest.

Could it be or was Lizzie imagining something more in Emma's expression?

"Keep walking," Caleb encouraged.

She glanced ahead at Ruben and hurried to catch up, almost tripping on a small step that led to the stage area.

Once she regained her balance and took her place on the dais, she glanced at Emma again.

Her lips had curved into the slightest of smiles and there was a twinkle in her eyes that Lizzie could see even from this distance.

Then Emma winked.

Lizzie wanted to laugh with joy, but the program coordinator was introducing the singers and prompting them to begin their first song.

In her enthusiasm about Emma, a sheet of music dropped from Lizzie's hand, slid across the floor and stopped at the table where Thad Thompson sat.

Lizzie's heart nearly jolted out of her chest. Retrieving her music would draw attention to herself, and without doubt, Thompson would recognize her. She hesitated for a long heart-wrenching moment, unsure of what to do.

TWENTY-EIGHT

Caleb groaned inwardly. Before he could retrieve Lizzie's fallen music, Ruben handed Lizzie his own music sheets. Then with a great deal of poise and finesse, he stepped forward and bowed to the head table in the fashion of Old England. As he bent down, he retrieved the elusive music, then returned to his spot and commenced to sing the opening solo. His voice was rich, and all eyes turned to him without noticing Lizzie and Caleb in the rear.

As Ruben sang, Lizzie let out an almost imperceptible sigh of relief. Caleb dropped his hand to where hers hung at her side and touched her fingers ever so slightly, hoping to offer support and encouragement. Out of the corner of his eye, he saw her ashen face and feared that if she did not regain her composure, she might collapse.

She gripped his hand for a moment, and then, as if buoyed by his presence, the color began to return to her cheeks.

Grateful that Ruben's deep, rich voice captured the audience's attention, Caleb turned his gaze to Emma. Lizzie was right. Although thinner and with her hair hanging around her slender face, there was no doubt who the woman was. She caught Caleb's gaze and nodded ever so slightly.

Once the first song ended, the program director introduced the head of the symposium who had high praise for this year's award recipient. Thad Thompson straightened his shoulders and appeared to puff out his chest as the words of commendation were spoken.

His brother-in-law, Warren Whitaker, seemed wary. He flicked his gaze around the room as if worried that his wrongdoings would be revealed at any moment.

Caleb felt a sense of impending uneasiness, as well.

Thad Thompson was invited to the podium. He was given another plaque from the chair of the symposium. "To hang in your office," the chairman said.

With a feigned smile of humility, Thompson accepted the plaque and offered his thanks, as well as gratitude for all who worked with him in ensuring folks in rural Georgia and the entire Southeast were provided with excellent resources for their rehab and long-term residential care. He also expressed his thanks to all who attended the event and to the carolers who would continue the program with more songs.

Relieved that the Florida manipulator seemed unaware of Lizzie's presence, Caleb joined in the singing. Toward the end of the final Christmas medley, the carolers promenaded round the tables where the handicapped children and adults were seated.

Caleb and Lizzie halted behind Emma's chair. The mix of Christmas favorites was joyous and upbeat, and at its conclusion, people from the rehab center presented each of the children and residential guests with a wrapped package.

The children's excitement was spontaneous. They tore off the wrapping paper and squealed at the gifts. The adults were enthused as well, and each person seemed grateful.

The chairman of the symposium neared Thad Thompson and his brother-in-law and shook their hands. The program director moved to the podium.

"This concludes our formal program. Please continue to enjoy yourselves for as long as you can stay."

Caleb nodded to Lizzie.

She tapped Emma's shoulder and leaned close to whisper in her ear. Emma nodded.

Lizzie left through a rear door. Emma slipped from her chair and followed her.

Caleb studied the crowd. No one seemed to have noticed their departure.

He glanced out the window and his stomach soured. Two police squad cars pulled to a stop in front of the complex. The officers climbed from their cars and headed toward the rehab center.

If Lizzie and Emma left the rehab center now, they would run into law enforcement. Caleb needed to warn them, but he was hemmed in behind two wheelchairs. One thing was certain, all their plans would end if Lizzie and Emma were discovered.

Lizzie waited in the hallway for Emma and grabbed her hand when she hurried from the dining room.

"Emma, do you recognize me today?"

"Oh, Lizzie, I knew you yesterday but was fearful due to the medication. Last night, I pretended to take my pills and then spit them out. This morning, I did the same. My confusion has started to ease. Yes, I know you, my dearest friend."

The women hugged briefly. "We must hurry, Emma. There is a wagon outside. You can hide there."

They started toward the door, but Lizzie stopped short. Two police officers were approaching the rehab center. She pulled Emma back away from the entrance area and secreted her behind a large, free-standing sign that bid a Merry Christmas and Happy New Year to all.

Lizzie's heart pounded nearly out of her chest. She held Emma's hand tightly and put a finger to her lips to ensure she knew to keep quiet.

The sound of the outside door opening and closing increased Lizzie's pulse.

Please, let us remain unseen, she silently prayed.

The two officers walked along the main corridor. Peering from behind the sign, Lizzie watched them enter the dining room. The enthusiastic chatter of the guests spilled into the hallway.

"Let's go." Lizzie motioned Emma toward the door. Glancing back, Lizzie was relieved to see that no one had followed them.

She opened the door and hurried Emma into the cool sunlight. "The wagon is at the side of the building."

The women hurried along the sidewalk. Ruben stood by one of the wagons.

"How did you get away?" Lizzie asked.

"I left as soon as you did but went in the opposite direction. There is a back door."

"Where's Caleb?"

"Still inside."

"He needs to be with us," she insisted.

"We'll give him a minute or two."

He turned his gaze to Emma and took her hand. "I tried to find you."

"They would not let me call anyone. I knew you would worry."

"Hurry," Lizzie insisted. "We can talk later."

Ruben lifted Emma into the wagon and helped Lizzie climb in, as well. They rearranged the bales of hay to provide a hiding spot in the center large enough for Emma to sit unnoticed.

"I'll throw a blanket over your secret hideaway so you will not be seen," Lizzie explained. "Make sure you have enough room."

"I'm fine," Emma whispered back to her once she had settled in.

Lizzie looked back at the rehab center. Where was Caleb?

"We need to leave now," Ruben said. He reached for the reins.

What could be keeping Caleb? Had the police found him, or had Thompson realized who he was?

Her mouth went dry and her pulse raced. She glanced at the police cars and the dark clouds rolling across the sky. If a storm hit, the festivities would be shut down, which would ruin their escape.

"We have to leave now," Ruben said again.

She refused to abandon Caleb. "One more minute," she pleaded.

Please, Gott, she silently prayed.

Ruben flicked the reins. "It is time."

At that moment, the side door opened and Caleb ran toward them. Lizzie stretched out her hand. He grasped it and hopped onto the wagon.

She nearly collapsed with relief. "I didn't think you would make it."

"The police were checking everyone at the door. One of the officers got tied up taking pictures with the children. That gave me an opportunity to leave without being noticed."

The guests at the luncheon began to spill out

of the rehab center. The children waved at the wagon as it passed.

Caleb and Lizzie waved back.

"Where's Emma?" he asked.

Lizzie glanced at the blanket stretched across the bales of hay.

"Is she all right?"

"She recognized me, Caleb, and admitted that she had not swallowed her pills last night or this morning. Although she has much to heal, she seemed more like her old self."

He nodded. "If only we can get her out of town."

Lizzie was optimistic. The worst was over. Emma was with them.

Glancing back, a weight fell on her shoulders. Both police officers hurried outside. They jumped into their cars and screeched out of the parking area, heading toward town on the same road the wagon was traveling.

If they stopped the wagon, Emma would be found and apprehended.

She glanced forward and gasped. A sports car convertible screeched around the corner and accelerated, heading toward the rehab center's campus. Her heart pounded so hard she feared it would beat out of her chest. The police caused her concern. They could arrest her and haul her back to Florida, but Andrew was a bigger threat. Once he had Emma and Lizzie in his clutches, Andrew would kill both of them.

TWENTY-NINE

The scream of the police sirens made Caleb's heart hammer in his chest. The two squad cars were gaining on them. Lizzie face was blanched and her eyes wide with worry as Andrew raced past them in his sports car. If only the self-absorbed playboy would remain at the rehab center with his father and uncle until Emma was back at Aunt Martha and Uncle Zach's house where, hopefully, she would be safe from danger.

Ruben glanced back at Caleb. "What do you want me to do about the police?"

"Pull over."

Lizzie grabbed his arm. "They'll search the wagon and find Emma. Andrew could turn around. Who knows what will happen if he sees her."

"Pray, Lizzie, that the cops don't find her."

He glanced over his shoulder. "Andrew must be with his father. If only all of them remain at the rehab center."

She lowered her head and closed her eyes. He hoped *Gott* heard Lizzie's prayer.

Ruben steered the buggy to the side of the road.

The police cars pulled up behind them. The driver of the lead car jumped out and approached the wagon. He eyed their costumes and the propped up bales of hay.

"Is there a problem?" Ruben asked.

"One of the women from the group home has gone missing."

"Perhaps she was in the restroom," Caleb suggested. "Or on the grounds, enjoying the lovely surroundings."

"Sir, we're searching the buildings and the expansive campus."

The officer turned his attention back to Ruben. "You want to explain why you left the center ahead of the other carolers?"

"In case you didn't notice, officer, there were two wagons. The rest of the group will follow shortly, but we are late for a singing at the far end of town. The event will be televised."

The cop turned to Caleb. "Have you seen anyone on the street who was at the luncheon?"

"We have seen no one." Glancing at Lizzie, he noticed the side of the blanket had caught in the wind and was lifting off the bales of hay.

Lizzie hazily lowered herself onto the hay and placed her hand on the shifting blanket.

"It is good to sit after the long morning," she said with a huff.

The cop raised his brow. "Are you feeling okay, ma'am?"

Lizzie looked like she was ready to collapse. She fanned her face and offered the officer a weak smile.

"A bit of motion sickness that will pass in a moment."

"You want me to take you to the doc's office, ma'am? See if he can give you something?"

Her gaze was filled with heartfelt gratitude. "That is so kind, but I will be fine. The fresh air is making me better already. You have work to do. We do not want to hold you up."

"Then we'll let you folks be on your way. Contact our headquarters if you see a frail young woman wandering the streets. She's had some mental problems, and the director is worried she has wandered off."

"I will pray for her safety."

"You do that, ma'am, and take care of yourself."

"Thank you, Officer."

The cop returned to his squad car and the two police vehicles headed down a side street and then turned toward the rehab center at the next block.

Lizzie glanced back again. "Do you see Andrew's car?"

Caleb shook his head. "Let's hope he remains at the rehab center."

She adjusted the blanket and glanced back again as Ruben encouraged the horses onto the road. As they neared the downtown area, the people on the sidewalks stopped to wave. A large bucket of individually wrapped candy sat on the floor of the wagon. She grabbed a handful and threw it to the crowd.

Ruben began to sing, his voice strong and melodious.

Caleb glanced over his shoulder. The street behind them seemed free from anyone out to do them harm.

"We're almost to the hotel," he said with relief.

Lizzie grabbed his hand.

"What's wrong?" He followed her gaze to the road ahead and groaned. A big guy with dark brown hair stood by a convertible sports car.

Caleb's gut tightened. Andrew Thompson must have taken a back road out of the rehab center in order to cut them off on Broad Street. Caleb had been naive to think he could outsmart such a hateful man. No matter what happened, he had to protect not only Emma but also Lizzie. Andrew Thompson wanted both of them dead.

Lizzie's pulse raced and her hands trembled.

"He's a fool," Caleb said. "And a drunk."

Andrew was walking in the middle of the street, waving his arms as if trying to spook the horses.

Ruben struggled with the reins. "Whoa, there. Calm down, girls. Everything's okay."

But it wasn't okay. The horses' heads were high, their ears forward.

"Come on, Sweetpea. Easy, Sugar." Ruben's calming voice did little to comfort the team.

"Keep going," Caleb told Ruben.

"No!" Lizzie's gut tightened. "You'll run him over."

"He'll jump clear," Caleb assured her. "Andrew wants to play chicken, but he's a coward."

"In that case, two can play this game." Ruben flicked the reins. "Let's go, Sugar. Pick up the pace, Sweetpea."

The horses increased their speed.

Lizzie gasped, unsure what would happen.

At the last moment, Andrew jumped to safety.

The wagon raced past him.

The hotel appeared in the distance. A TV van was parked at the side of the road. Jeb and Harold were being interviewed by the television anchorman.

"The Chevy you rented is parked behind the hotel," Lizzie told Caleb. "Would we be safer taking the car?"

"We don't have time to stop. Jeb and Harold will alert the authorities."

The authorities—meaning the police—would arrest her. At least, Emma would be safe in law enforcement's care.

Glancing back, Lizzie felt a swell of relief. Andrew hadn't followed them. Maybe Caleb was right. Remaining in the wagon would hasten their escape.

Minutes later, her optimism plummeted when the roar of a sports car sounded behind them. Andrew was following them. He raised a gun over the top of the windshield and fired.

People screamed and ran into the shops. Other folks dove for cover behind benches.

"Clear the streets," someone cried.

More gunfire.

"Get down, Lizzie." Caleb's voice.

She dropped to the floor of the wagon.

Emma whimpered.

"Everything's okay," Lizzie tried to assure her. But it wasn't okay to have Andrew closing in on them. He had a weapon, and he was *liquored up*, as Mr. Thompson's housekeeper had said.

"He wants to kill me," Emma cried.

"We won't let anyone hurt you again." That was Lizzie's prayer. *Please,* Gott, *keep Emma safe*.

Another round of fire. A bullet hit the back of the wagon. Too close.

Ruben flicked the reins. "We're leaving town and heading onto the main road."

The wagon was going full speed. Emma crawled from her hiding place and laid next to Lizzie.

She grabbed Emma's hand and held on.

Peering into the distance, Lizzie's stomach rolled.

"There's a sharp bend ahead. The horses are going too fast."

"Rein in the team," Caleb yelled to Ruben.

"They're bolting," he called back. "Hang on."

The horses raced around the bend. The wagon shimmied back and forth. The rear wheel bounced onto the berm and slid into a ditch. The horses dragged the wagon until it jolted to a stop, sending everything and everyone crashing to the ground.

Lizzie screamed as she landed with a *thump*, momentarily stunned.

Caleb! She scrambled to her feet and ran to where he lay.

"Get up." She tugged on his arm, but he failed to respond.

"Please, *Gott*!"

Placing her fingers on his neck, she felt for a pulse. Then moved her fingers again.

A faint pulse. Too faint.

Tears burned her eyes.

She spied Ruben sprawled on the ground not far from the horses who appeared uninjured. She tried to raise him, but to no avail.

Where was Emma? Before she could find her friend, Andrew's sports car screeched to a stop. He stumbled to the pavement, gun raised, and fired a shot into the air.

She flinched.

His eyes widened when he saw her. He pointed

to the bandage on his neck. "It's payback time. You and Emma are leaving with me."

"She's not here, Andrew." At least, Lizzie hadn't seen her.

Keep her alive, Gott. *Please!*

Andrew glanced at the tilted wagon, the spilled bales of hay and the two men whose limp bodies tore a hole in Lizzie's heart.

"You're the reason all this happened." He stepped toward her and narrowed his gaze. His breath smelled of alcohol. "You came on to me that day on the beach and said you'd meet me that night, but you sent your stupid blond girlfriend instead."

His face twisted. "Blondes remind me of my mother. She said she loved me, but she loved Thad Thompson's money more. That's why I had to teach your friend a lesson."

"You're a hateful man."

He threw back his head and laughed. "That's not what you thought that day at the beach. You said the guy you cared about was marrying your best friend so you agreed to meet me later that night."

"I didn't know what I was saying."

"You stood me up and sent your friend instead. When she rejected me, I got mad."

"I was waiting at the edge of the beach, but you didn't see me because you were more interested in Emma. You almost killed her and then kept her drugged up for three years. The authorities already know."

"You're lying."

He grabbed her throat with one hand and started to choke her just as he had done at his father's estate.

"This time you'll die." He raised the gun to her head.

She gasped for air and struggled to break free.

Out of the corner of her eye, she saw Caleb's leg move. Relief swept over her, although if Andrew had his way, they'd all end up dead.

She pounded her fists against his chest and struggled to jerk free from his hold, all the while her gaze was on Caleb.

He rolled to his side and started to rise.

Andrew heard him and turned. In that instant, she jammed her fingers into his neck exactly where the letter opener had cut into his flesh in Mr. Thompson's office.

He shrieked with pain and reeled.

Caleb grabbed Andrew's leg and threw him to the ground. He landed on his back. Air *whooshed* from his lungs. The weapon flew from his hand.

Groaning, he rolled over and climbed to his feet.

Caleb was faster. He lunged headlong into Andrew and knocked him off balance.

With a groan, Andrew staggered forward and

slammed into the backside of the nearest of the two mares.

Sweetpea snorted, then raised her rump and kicked. Her hoof caught Andrew in the gut. He doubled over and moaned.

The mare kicked again.

Andrew flailed his arms and became entangled in the harness. The mare reared, throwing him into the air. He crashed to the ground under her hooves.

Lizzie grabbed the reins. "Whoa, girl. Whoa." With a soothing voice, she tried to calm the frantic horse.

Caleb took the reins and eased the team back.

Andrew lay motionless on the ground. He had a gash on his forehead, and he was bleeding from his neck and mouth. His shoulder appeared dislocated, and his eyes were glazed over.

Caleb knelt beside him and felt for a pulse. "He's not breathing."

Lizzie dropped to her knees beside them.

Caleb wrapped his hands together and pushed on Andrew's chest in a series of rapid compressions.

"Stay with us, Andrew," she whispered. "Please, *Gott*." As terrible as he was, she didn't want Andrew to die.

Sirens sounded in the distance. Help was coming, but Lizzie wasn't sure it would arrive in time.

Jeb and the AJC reporter pulled up behind the

wagon and parked on the side of the road. A van, bearing a television logo, screeched to a stop. The cameraman leaned out the window and started rolling.

Lizzie held up her hand. "Not now. This man's injured. He needs help."

Jeb hurried forward and knelt beside Caleb. "We called the ambulance when we saw you race by in town."

Lizzie ran to where Emma lay half hidden between a bale of hay and the brush at the side of the road. She wiped the hair from her face. "Emma, can you hear me? You're going to be okay."

But Lizzie wasn't sure her friend would survive. She had been attacked three years ago, held captive and then escaped only to be injured again.

Emma didn't have a chance. All because of Lizzie. Tears rolled from her eyes.

The ambulance pulled to a stop. A pair of EMTs tended to Andrew. A third man hurried to help Emma. He checked for a pulse, then broke a vial of smelling salts and held it under her nose. She jerked awake.

"Emma, can you hear me?" Lizzie said.

Her friend blinked her eyes open and smiled. "Are…are you all right, Lizzie?"

"I'm fine."

"What about Ruben?"

Like Caleb, he had been knocked out. "The

EMTs are caring for him, but he doesn't seem to want their help."

"And Caleb?"

"He's talking to one of the police officers." Although she knew that the EMTs would check his condition later.

Lizzie looked at the scene of the wreck and realized what Andrew said was true. She was responsible for everything that had happened.

She approached the nearest officer and held out her hands. "Arrest me. This is all my fault."

"Ma'am, you hit your head. I'll have an EMT look at you next."

No one believed her. But what did it matter? Emma was safe and at long last she and Caleb would be together.

THIRTY

When Caleb was released from the hospital later that night, Lizzie was waiting for him.

"Aunt Martha and Uncle Zach are worried about you," she told him.

"The doc said I pulled a few muscles and probably had the air knocked out of me. Nothing serious or life-threatening."

"I thought you were dead."

"For a second, I thought I was too."

"The doctor released Emma earlier. Ruben took her to your aunt and uncle's house."

"Any information on Andrew?" Caleb asked.

"He's been transported to a hospital in Atlanta. His condition is critical. If he does recover, he'll have a lengthy rehabilitation."

"In one of his father's facilities?"

Lizzie smiled sadly.

"What about Thad Thompson?" Caleb asked.

"He's being held without bail, along with his brother-in-law. A few of the nurses at Respite Haven saw more than they ever let on. They want to talk to the police."

Caleb sighed. "It sounds as if Jeb and Harold will get their big stories."

Lizzie nodded. "Much to Thad Thompson's displeasure."

The ride to his aunt and uncle's house took longer than Caleb had expected. When he pulled into the drive, Aunt Martha and Uncle Zach ran to greet both of them with hugs and sighs of relief.

"Ruben said you were knocked unconscious," his aunt shared.

"Short-term because of the fall from the wagon. The doctors checked me over. I'm fine."

"Emma is staying in the downstairs guest room," his uncle said.

"And Ruben?" Lizzie asked.

"He went home to tend to his animals."

Stepping into the kitchen, Caleb had a sense of homecoming. He touched Lizzie's arm, but she pulled away.

He moved closer. "There is so much I want to tell you."

She held up her hand to quiet him. "Not now, Caleb. Emma's waiting for you. I know you have a lot to discuss."

"But—"

"I'm going upstairs so you can have privacy."

"Don't go, Lizzie. Stay here."

She shook her head. "I'll see you later."

Later was not what he wanted, as he watched her leave, but if she wanted him to talk to Emma, he would do just that.

He knocked on the guest-room door and stepped inside, unsure of how to say what was heavy on his heart.

* * *

Lizzie sat on the bed with her head in her hands, thinking of where she would go next. Back to Amish Mountain more than likely, although she had hoped to hear from her family by now.

Emma and Caleb would probably make their home in Pinecraft. If so, Lizzie might remain in the Freemont area. Caleb's aunt and uncle seemed to want her to stay, although her heart would be heavy without Caleb.

A knock sounded at the bedroom door.

"Enter, please." She wiped her hand over her cheeks to dry her tears.

Aunt Martha stepped into the room.

"Is everything okay?" Lizzie asked.

"The evening meal is ready. I had hoped you would join us."

"I'll stay upstairs tonight. Tell Emma and Caleb good-night for me."

"I will tell Emma, but Caleb has gone."

"Gone?"

"He is driving back to Pinecraft."

"What about Emma?"

"She is handling everything quite well. Ruben came back and is staying for dinner."

"Ruben?"

"He is a *gut* man."

Lizzie did not understand what Aunt Martha was saying. "Ruben and Emma?"

"It is something I suspected when I heard of

Ruben's attentiveness to her needs at the Haven. Emma must heal, but there is a bond between them." Aunt Martha shrugged ever so slightly. "Time will tell, *yah*?"

"He is older."

"By only a few years." Martha smiled. "Zachariah is six years my senior, yet age is not a deciding factor with love."

Love? "What about Caleb?"

"He told Emma on the day you went to the beach that he did not have feelings for her."

"She never said anything to me."

"Perhaps she was hurt. Caleb suspected she met Andrew that night on the rebound because he had broken off the relationship she thought they had."

"But, Aunt Martha—" Lizzie needed to explain what really had happened. "Emma went to the beach that night because I introduced her to Andrew. *I* was the one who started it all. I knew Emma and Caleb would marry. I was feeling sorry for myself and wanted someone to notice me."

"Someone has been noticing you, dear."

Lizzie did not know what Aunt Martha meant, but she was too upset to ask. She wanted to go to bed, close her eyes and pretend none of this had happened. She hoped the morning would bring clarity about her future. Perhaps she would go back to cleaning homes. It was honorable work and provided an income.

One thing was certain—she would not go back to Pinecraft. There were too many memories there.

THIRTY-ONE

On Christmas morn, Lizzie helped Aunt Martha with the cooking. Chickens roasted in the oven along with heaping casseroles of stuffing and sweet potatoes. Cooked green beans and mashed potatoes warmed on the stove, and an assortment of gelatin molds and colorful salads lined the counter. Throughout the week, they had baked pies and cakes and made an assortment of candies that awaited the noonday meal.

After breakfast, Uncle Zach had read the Nativity passage from Scripture aloud before hurrying outside to complete his chores.

Ruben had arrived a few hours later to take Emma on a buggy ride before the Christmas meal. Her memory had not returned fully and she was still confused at times and had difficulty with some large motor functions, but the twinkle in her eyes warmed Lizzie's heart.

She was still waiting for the letter from her family.

Perhaps it would never come. If not, she would try to find someplace to live, hopefully not too far from Aunt Martha and Uncle Zach.

The sound of an automobile on the drive drew her to the window. Her heart thudded against her chest.

"It's Caleb, Aunt Martha, in the rental car. He's come back to see you and Uncle Zach."

"Such a *wunderbaar* Christmas surprise. Go outside and greet him, dear. Tell him he is in time for our Christmas meal."

"You greet him, Martha. He doesn't want to see me."

"Such foolish talk." The older woman tsked and shooed her toward the door. "You are old friends, Lizzie. You need to iron out any problems you have with one another."

"I don't have a problem." *Far from it.*

"Go, dear, so he knows he's welcome."

Lizzie opened the door and stepped onto the porch. The sun was high in the sky and the day was mild in spite of the time of year.

The car came to a stop and Caleb stepped out. He was dressed Amish and seemed taller and much more handsome, if that could be. For a long moment, he stared at her with dark eyes that made her throat go dry and her pulse race. Slowly, his full lips curved into a warm smile.

"*Frehlicher Grischtdagg*, Lizzie."

"Merry Christmas to you, Caleb. Your aunt has been cooking for days. You are in time to enjoy the delicious feast she has prepared."

"I missed you."

Surely she had not heard correctly. "Your aunt and uncle have missed you, as well."

He climbed the steps and stopped a few feet

from where she stood. Suddenly nervous and feeling unsure of herself, she held her hands together as her fingers played with the edge of her apron.

"What about you, Lizzie? Have you missed me?"

I have thought of you every second of every minute, she wanted to say. Instead, she steeled her spine and held her head high. "You and I have been friends for a long time, Caleb. It is *gut* to see you again."

"I had to go back to Pinecraft."

She nodded. "I understand. Your business is there."

"I turned it over to the manager of the neighboring store. She will run both shops until the owner finds a replacement for me."

Lizzie was surprised by his comment. "You are not staying in Pinecraft?"

"Everyone I care about is in Georgia."

"Aunt Martha and Uncle Zach will be glad to hear your plans."

"I love them dearly, but I did not come back because of them." He stepped closer and reached for her hand.

She hesitated and then allowed him to wrap his fingers through hers. Warmth flooded over her.

"I came back to be with you, Lizzie."

Her heart nearly stopped. "What are you saying?"

"I'm saying, growing up you were the strong one, the energetic one, the one who knew what to do and when to do it."

"Did you not hear what I said to Andrew?"

"I know you introduced yourself to him on the beach. You always were outgoing and friendly."

She pulled her hand away. "I wanted more than a friendship, Caleb. I wanted a boyfriend, only I chose the worst possible person. I wasn't thinking with my head that day. I was thinking with my heart. My broken heart."

"Oh, Lizzie—"

"I knew you and Emma were marrying when we returned to Willkommen. I wanted someone to love me, as well."

"But I did not want to marry Emma. At the time, I was not thinking of taking a wife, but ever since you appeared on my doorstep and we have been together, it's become more and more obvious that the feelings I always had for you were more than friendship. They started as that, but grew into love. *Like a strong vine that holds a marriage together*, you told me in the kitchen in Pinecraft."

"Oh, Caleb." There was a roaring in her ears, and she did not think her knees would hold her upright. Surely she was dreaming and would soon awake to learn that none of this was real.

He stepped closer. His right hand touched her

cheek. She stared into his eyes, and the world stood still.

His lips lowered and gently brushed against hers.

A delicious warmth coursed through her. He pulled her closer and again their lips met, this time with a rush of intensity that made her head spin and her heart nearly burst with joy. She folded more deeply into his arms and enjoyed the feel of him as he kissed her again and again.

He pulled back ever so slightly. "I talked to the bishop about baptism."

"You want to be Amish again?"

"I do. Then I want to court you, Lizzie, and marry you. I want to live wherever you want, perhaps here near my aunt and uncle. I've been doing more carving and contacted a few of the shop owners in Warm Springs. They would like to take my work on consignment at first."

"You'll have your own shop someday."

"Perhaps, but I want to farm the land. My land. Our land. I want it all, Lizzie. I want you, I want children, I want a farm, I want to carve wood and whittle on the side, and I want to remain Amish to raise a family in the community where *Gott* is first and family is a close second. Where neighbors reach out to one another and offer help in times of need. Where hard work brings satisfaction and where love flows between a man and a woman, equally yoked. This is what I want.

I want a partner who stands with me instead of walking behind me. I want a woman who knows her mind and isn't afraid to do what is right. Not just any woman, Lizzie. I want you as my wife."

He stared into her eyes. "I love you. I always have and I always will."

"Oh, Caleb. I love you, and yes, I want to marry you. Wherever you want to live will make me happy, but a home in this area would be a blessing for not only us but also for your aunt and uncle."

He kissed her again until they both started laughing with pure joy. The pain of the past had been replaced with the expectation of a wonderful life together.

"I made something for you." He squeezed her hand and retrieved a small wrapped box from the car.

"A Christmas present?" she asked, her heart beating even faster.

"A forever present."

She removed the wrapping and sighed with delight at the small wooden box decorated with two entwined hearts. A small cross was carved into the upper left-hand quadrants of each heart.

"Remember how we used to say *cross my heart* as a promise statement when we were young?"

She nodded. "I do remember."

"This box is my promise statement to you,

Lizzie, that I will love you forever. Cross my heart."

Her first name was carved across the top, like the plaques in Caleb's shop. She rubbed her finger over an empty space at the bottom. "What goes here?"

He smiled sheepishly. "Any name you choose."

"I want your name there, Caleb. Will you carve it for me?"

He nodded. "I'll have it ready by Old Christmas."

The Epiphany when the Magi presented gifts to the King of Kings.

"Oh, Caleb." Lizzie sighed, upset with her own failure. "I… I do not have a gift for you."

His eyes twinkled and his mouth turned into a luscious grin. "Sweet Lizzie, you are my gift. You are all I have ever wanted."

Her heart soared as they walked arm in arm into the kitchen. They didn't need to tell Aunt Martha what had transpired. She could read the joy on their faces. Uncle Zach could as well when he came in from the barn.

Later that day, as they gathered around the Christmas table, along with Emma and Ruben, and lowered their heads in prayer, Lizzie gave thanks for finding not only her missing friend but also the man she loved.

Just as she had told Caleb in Pinecraft, love was the vine that would hold their marriage together. The seed had been planted long ago, and although their paths had parted for a period of time, *Gott* had brought Caleb and Lizzie back together. Sometimes love took time to discover, but after everything that had happened, Lizzie realized true love can never be denied.

* * * * *

If you enjoyed this story, look for these other books by Debby Giusti:

Her Forgotten Amish Past
Dangerous Amish Inheritance

Dear Reader,

I hope you enjoyed *Amish Christmas Search*. Lizzie Kauffman's best friend, Emma, has gone missing, and Lizzie will do anything to find her, even strike out on her own in Pinecraft, Florida, an Amish vacation spot. But investigating Emma's disappearance puts Lizzie in danger and the only person who can help is Caleb Zook, the man Emma planned to marry. Their unlikely alliance takes them on a deadly journey that threatens not only Lizzie's life but also her heart.

I pray for my readers each day and would love to hear from you. Email me at debby@debbygiusti.com or write me c/o Love Inspired, 195 Broadway, 24th Floor, New York, NY 10007. Visit me at www.debbygiusti.com and at www.facebook.com/debby.giusti.9.

As always, I thank God for bringing us together through this story.

Wishing you abundant blessings,
Debby